TANABATA

~~~~~~~~~~~~~~~~~~~~~~~~

a novel

by
Miles Hitchcock

ISBN 978-1-257-79097-5

Cover photography courtesy of
www.photos8.com

Contents

A Grandfather's Tale

The Marco Polo Bridge

The Origin of the Years

Big Ears

The Golden Lion Snack Bar

The Dig

The Teahouse Scroll

The Satellite Launch

The Cosmonaut's Tale

The Imperial Palace

This novel is dedicated
to the city of Kyoto, Japan
and its people.

A Grandfather's Tale

All along the river, fireworks are burning. Children are running up and down the banks, like fireflies circling and zigzagging between the trees. My grandchildren are breathless, clutching sparklers.

"Why are you wearing tails grandpa?"

"Because I'm off to meet the Emperor!"

They laugh and grab rice balls and watermelon, and run off to light firecrackers under the bridge. I lean back in my chair and look up – the stars are running like a river through the sky, and I spot Vega and Altair – two bright points in the twilight. Tonight is the festival of Tanabata, when these two stars are able to meet after a year of abstinence. From here on Earth it appears they take light-year steps across the galaxy to become lovers embracing under a secret arch of night.

"Do you want to hear my version of the Tanabata story?" I ask the children on their next run around. "Yes grandpa Ambrose!" They shout. My sons and daughters roll their eyes because I do this every year – dress up in my old-fashioned tails and tell the same old story - but still the youngest children run to listen.

"A long time ago, before this city was built, and before this river even ran past this spot, a fairy fell in love with a farmer who owned the field right here where we sit." We pause and look around. "The fairy lived in that hill over there," I point across the river to Kirin Shrine, an ancient grove sandwiched between apartment blocks and showrooms.

"Now listen children, fairies find humans to be fairly stupid creatures, cruel with selfish desires - but this farmer was very gentle and handsome, and every night the fairy came to the forest's edge to admire his beauty, and sing the most beautiful, magical songs to him. The farmer crept out of his cottage, entranced by her voice and elegance - he knew that not many men were so lucky to attract the fancy of a gorgeous fairy - and was only too happy to follow her into the woods. Soon they were spending the evening in each other's arms. The fairy's mother flew into a rage, for it is forbidden for fairies to marry humans, and with a fierce spell she changed the course of the river to flow between the farmer's fields and the wood, washing away his best fields, and separating him from his lover. But the fairy kept singing – the songs now painfully broken and sad, as she flitted in the moonlight along the river shore – and he listened heartbroken from his cottage, weeping and pining.

"This carried on for a year until the magpies who lived in the farmer's fields took pity on them. One summer's evening, when the river was calm after the monsoon floods, and the farmer rested beside the green rice crops, the King of the Magpies called all of the birds to his fields, so the couple could meet. Millions of magpies flew from all over the world, out of the mountains and forests, over seas from distant isles, to descend in a giant black cloud. But they did not devour the farmer's crop; they bridged the river, making a feathery arch to enclose the lovers, who walked gingerly over their pied backs.

"With tears of love and pleasure the fairy and the farmer lay down in their avian bed, hidden from the sight of the fairy's mother, and their joyful cries were muted by the cooing and cawing of the birds. So true love was found and even now, once a year, you can still hear the King of the Magpies calling, and you might even see the feathery bridge, and the farmer and fairy surrounded by fluttering, cooing birds, embracing in its midst."

I usually whisper at this point, and cock an ear toward the river. "Listen closely children, can you hear the flapping of wings, and the magic notes of the fairy's song? If you squint your eyes in the right way, you might see a magical bridge of light fluttering across this river, soft amongst the shadows of the city and the glittering reflections of the Tanabata stars."

The youngest are sitting with half-closed eyes now, listening hopefully, swaying in their seats, until their mother claps and passes around sweet bean cakes. But the spell has been cast. It was not just for the children I told the story: I am back beside another magical bridge long ago, watching the fireflies circle on the banks, and the fireworks arch overhead.

The Marco Polo Bridge

Borders are, true to their nature, two-dimensional – you can change your point of view and they disappear. Take Korea, Palestine, Tibet: depending on who you speak to, these countries exist in different places. The occupied zones have different names, the North and South partitions are defined by different borders. Rockets and propaganda crisscross these lines, blurring them with rubble, obscuring them with fog. Walls are built over shared fields and roads, between parents and children, memories and loyalties.

The same goes for borders in time – change your perspective and they disappear. Most schoolbooks mark the commencement of the Patriotic War with the bombing of Hanoi, but in this part of the world that ridiculous raid was the disastrous mid-point of an entirely different war. The Patriotic War began twelve years before Hanoi, on July 7 - the night of Tanabata - in Year Twelve of the Shining Path Emperor, under the Marco Polo Bridge in Xian. I know the exact moment because I started it.

I was a seventeen-year-old private with the Seventh Imperial Army. The Empire's borders were quickly zigzagging through East Asia. The September 18 Incident had taken place a year before, changing the geopolitical landscape. That event brought our foot thudding down onto the Asian mainland, and we weren't about to turn back. On 11/9/18, Red Army terrorists destroyed Manchuria's steel plants and rail lines, crippling the oil-rich state. By the terms of our alliance we were forced to intervene. It is now a recorded fact that not just the communists but three national intelligence agencies were involved, including ours. The event was engineered to benefit several competing interests. After Manchuria, we occupied the provinces of Formosa and Xian. The strategy: invade the Siberian oilfields and wrong-foot the Americans. It held. We appeared to be unstoppable; but then came Tanabata, and my mistake.

My division was stationed on the west bank of the Yongdao River. On the east side of the river was a large Kuomintang garrison. The position was technically front line, but a truce had held for years, as each side got on with the business of tackling the common foes: communism and colonialism.

The two armies were separated by the Marco Polo Bridge, an ancient kilometre of stone arches built nine hundred years before, near the limit of the famous Venetian's eastern wanderings. It was constructed from the red mud brick characteristic of most medieval monuments, and connected Xian with its vast and long-disputed territories. It has been crossed by the armies of every nation, by victorious kings and exiled Emperors, by great merchants and enlightened saints, by every technology known to man and products from every country. Every species and every grain of knowledge has at one time been funneled between its pillars, on each of which roars a great lion, eroded into toothless age by the centuries.

So in Year 12 I was stationed beside it, fresh out of basic training, patriotic yet grateful to have found such a safe post. The great bridge was a symbol of truce – around it spread tent cities and fortifications. Grey airships floated above: radio towers and guys for cables and kites which defended it from dive bombers. The bridge was a shared resource, a firm handshake that stretched between not just two armies but two civilisations. The air crackled with loudspeakers and the buzz of diesel trucks delivering supplies to thousands of restive soldiers.

By the time of my posting there, army life had settled into the boring and eventless passing of hours common to working truces the world over: teenage boys roaming the towns and fields with nothing to do but drink, play cards, and harass the local girls. We cleaned our weapons and boots with spotless precision. We held regular drills and patrols, and made supply runs to the coast. We wrote letters, read dirty magazines and shot stray dogs for target practice. A black market trade was run by and for the officers, but we rarely had enough money for it, so most of our clandestine exchange of cigarettes, pornography and alcohol was with our adversaries over the bridge.

Over time I became good friends with several Kuomintang soldiers. We soon picked up each other's words - we had a script in common - and when we met for games of handball and chance we talked long after, mainly about girls and combat, but also about the ideals and dreams fed to us by our superiors. One soldier was an officer-in-waiting called Hei-Jin. He was a firebrand: anti-Western and fiercely nationalist, like all of us at the time. Even though our rulers were different, Hei-Jin and I were basically the same. We came from the same ancient branches of language and blood. We both served under the auspices of a living god, our ancestor and Emperor, to liberate Asia: industrialise its economies, secure its oilfields, kick out the European exploiters. Back then, we and the KMT were not true enemies; there was none of the bad blood between our countries that exists today, a situation for which I hold myself personally responsible.

Hei-Jin and I liked to talk about what would happen after the Kuomintang defeated the communists – that our countries would join forces to keep America out of Asia and re-establish the original civilisation. We used to laugh at the European Reich – we already had one, we declared, and it was two and a half thousand years old. We'd march cross the Marco Polo bridge in our black boots, a bridge which in name and deed spanned centuries, continents and points of view. We'd scratch graffiti into its ancient stones, and stub out our cigarettes, waiting for the glories of victory - freedom, national destiny, racial purity. Foolish and dangerous ideas, yes, but then what war isn't based on them, and what seventeen year old doesn't entertain them?

And what seventeen year-old doesn't foolishly fall in love from afar, with someone impossible to reach?

Every morning traders from the local villages lined up on the bridge to carry fresh food and sweets into the army camps through checkpoints. The sellers were mainly girls who carried baskets of fruit and sweet rice across their shoulders, and it was our pastime, I admit, to harass these girls for favours. Their bribes were nothing special – a free lime, a pack of broken biscuits – but of course we asked for more; we groped and joked and made lewd comments; it helped us think of ourselves as men if we treated them as whores.

However, the first time I saw Mei Li I was struck dumb. And not just me – most of the boys fell for her superlative features. Amongst the round-faced, squat-legged peasant girls in the queue, her face had perfect symmetry; a thin, regal nose, cheek-bones so high they caught strands of her black hair – hair so thick it seemed alive, reflecting waves of silver. Yet when I sidled up to her for the first time in the queue, full of teenage bravado, my hopeful jeers were silenced: she hobbled past, prodded by the girls around her, one almond-shaped eye staring back at mine, and the other waving at the ground like a spring on a stick. She limped slowly on a club foot, and her right hand was a twist of fingers, bent in itself as if clutching a bird; many officers searched this clenched limb, prising apart the fixed bones to look for contraband, only to find them empty. Beautiful Mei Li was a cripple, a simpleton. She made wordless noises, and her one beautiful eye was glazed with indifference.

"Another one fallen under Mei-Li's spell," the girls jested. "Such a beautiful face could win a war. It turns brave soldiers to stone." The other boys mimicked her cross-eyed shuffle, or made revolting noises as she passed, but I couldn't abuse her; I remained, to my deep shame and confusion, intensely attracted to her. Every day I let her pass silently, my heart beating, letting the noisy cruelty of my peers camouflage my blushes. Nontheless, Mei Li noticed them, and soon freely offered me gifts – an orange or a sweet pressed into my palm with the elegant fingers of her good hand, fingers of such contrasting proportions to the others that they seemed carved by a master craftsman. With her gifts I also received the teasings of both Mei Li's peers and mine, but I was secretly pleased there was a heart and intelligence in that dumb body, and that I had revealed it.

I was soon to reveal far more about Mei Li.

Every Sunday I was assigned to assist my commanding officer, Yamamoto, in his quarters. I would make his breakfast, polish his boots and saddlery – officers still kept horses in that time - I would then go to the market for his private supplies: whisky and coffee, molasses, racy magazines.

On the morning of July 7 that year – Tanabata – as I did my duties, I noticed Mei Li standing in the square outside his quarters. The stall holders often used her to deliver items to the officers, as she was less likely to be harassed by the soldiers loitering around the camp. I gave her a friendly greeting – she looked startled, and shuffled off. Later, as I returned from the stables, I found Yamamoto's door ajar – I was sure I had closed it. I quietly peered inside and froze. Mei-Li was crouched in the corner of the room, reaching out for Yamamoto's sword, which stood on a low table.

Yamamoto was of warlord stock, and his sword had been forged by some long-dead ancestor. In his cups he would draw it and declare how he would honour his line by drenching it in foreign blood. It wasn't an unusual sentiment: we had not had a good war in two hundred years, and many officers from the old families carried their inherited swords onto the mainland solely for this purpose. It was a kind of craze. One newspaper even offered a substantial sum of money for the greatest number of heads taken by a single officer. Such were the times.

As I watched, she picked the weapon up, held it high, and began to withdraw it from its scabbard, studying the emerging steel with a curious expression of awe. Then she seemed to remember her haste. She re-sheathed the sword and concealed it in a receptacle under her skirts, then turned and ran with her prize toward the door. She ran, I noticed, without a club foot, without a slow swaying shuffle, and as her eyes met mine - both clear and focused and burning with sharp intent, crossed by shock and surprise as she skidded to a halt before me.

My reaction was furiously mixed and inappropriate for someone catching a thief – I felt cheated. Not by her crime, but by her perfection. My attraction to her defects had been my secret, but now they were gone, and I was confronted by an entirely different creature. This creature had the flawless beauty that had at first struck me dumb, yet with an added delinquence: treachery – a greater flaw than those it replaced. My heart experienced the unfamiliar wrench of unfaithfulness, and my immediate response was violent – I slapped her hard, on her high cheek; the cheek that pressed her eyes into their alluring curve.

She simultaneously stepped back and delivered a hard blow to my chest. The fight was on. This new Mei Li was no stranger to martial arts. I grappled with her wrist but she expertly twisted mine with her own, side-stepped me in a flash and was out of my grasp. I lunged and managed to grab a fistful of her hair. She twisted on the end of it for a moment, then used its tension to swing a kick into my belly. I fell, winded, but the blow spun her off balance, and she landed clumsily on a leg and an arm. I jumped desperately to grip her from behind and found the sword inside her dress - she grabbed it too. I wrenched it over her head, forcing her to spin her around to face me.

We were locked in an interesting position. Her hempen dress was twisted around her shoulders, restricting her arms, yet she gripped the sword. If I moved to gain further advantage, she could use the sword against me, but she couldn't move until I did. Was I prepared to use the sword against her? She stared at me, weighing my will.

I was terrified. Her eyes were lit by a cold fury. She was clearly a formidable opponent; a member of some well-trained group of brigands who had been infiltrating the enemy camp for months. I nearly called outside for help – but I knew my pride would be lost if I needed assistance to subdue a woman. I tried to push her backwards – she leant back on one leg, subtly changed her grip and held me fast. As her eyes bore into mine, she suddenly recognised me. "Ah! You are the boy that likes Mei Li." Her face broke into a smile. She then offered me a bribe, a gift: "If I let the sword go now, you will fall, kind soldier, and Mei Li can escape."

Her offer of truce was not a bad one under the circumstances. If the fight continued it would become lethal, yet she was asking for my collusion in her escape, which I could not give. There was a further unintended consequence of my maneuver: we were pressed face to face, breast to breast, and her belly warmed mine; I must admit a spear of lust forced its way through my fear and anger. As if stating my terms, I slowly wrapped one leg around hers.

She stared up at me as if I were a dog. Yet she too was a soldier, and could easily sense the greater weakness of her opponent. "You want to kiss Mei Lee," she stated, matter-of-factly. "If I know you won't cut me," she added, "you may kiss her. Kiss her, and don't tell a soul about me."

My clumsy lips bumped into hers. She could have easily delivered a terrible blow at that moment, and perhaps she didn't see my fear, because she slid her fingers behind my neck and surrounded my face in silver-black hair. As our tongues met, she prised my fingers from the sword and drew them lower down into her skirts. We kneeled on Yamamoto's futon, and within a few moments I knew a woman for the first time.

Looking back now, it was nothing but the rape of a captive; at best the self-interested coupling of soldier and whore. But we agreed, calculatingly, to transform our violence into intimacy, and on finding no borders between the two, we made some kind of love. But what was the cost of my virginity? If my theory of history is correct, it cost the fate of my country; the tyranny in the North, the occupation of the South, the complete division of the whole. If she had killed me right then, at my weakest and most stupid moment, none of this would have happened. But she didn't. She trembled in my embrace. There was kindness in our caresses and great joy in our abandon.

Years later when I saw her face on the Northern posters, that famous lithograph, I fell to my knees and felt her soft skin on mine. I still do. Of course you think I am a nostalgic fool, romanticizing about women and war while his grandchildren play around him in peace. But there is no peace here today. Just an ugly scar across my country, and another around my heart.

As soon as I fell from her she stood up, scooped up Yamamoto's sword and walked to the door, turning to me: "if you follow me, then I will kill you, at the cost of my life." With the skill of an actress and the air of a magician, her eye looped to the ground, her right hand turned into a talon, and she dragged her club foot outside. I stayed on the floor. Beside me lay her kanzashi – her hair comb with four teeth like a fork – which must have fallen during our exertions. I knew it would be the last time I would see her, so I picked it up as a memento – it had a chrysanthemum pattern, inlaid with mother-of-pearl.

*   *   *

That night a military exercise was planned. My unit was in a forward position near the bridge, awaiting orders. We were to practice defending the bridge during an enemy offensive, which involved sheltering in camouflaged tunnels under intense artillery bombardment, followed by a counter-offensive against an imaginary brigade crossing the river. The purpose of our position was to defend the bridge charges at all costs – ultimately a suicide mission. If we were over-run, it was my commander Yamamoto's role to blow the great brick monument into history.

Yamamoto had spent all day in the field and had yet to discover that his family sword was missing. I had reported everything present and accounted for after I had finished my duties. The lost sword would of course cause a fit of rage and a destructive search of nearby villages – it was inevitable – but I was terrified that I would face some form of exemplary discipline – a beating with a bamboo cane perhaps, or a few days in a cage - had I reported the loss. So I concealed my error.

The beginning of the exercise was delayed and instead of remaining in the tunnels we stood in the open, playing cards and smoking. I needed to relieve myself and, as it was dark, instead of using the bunker latrine I wandered to the river. I slid down the bank, clambered through a shadowy bamboo grove, and came to the riverbed.

The long stone curve of the bridge divided the starry sky. Fireflies looped and circled in the air like tiny green lamps. I squatted on the rocks listening to the water going past in a hiss. I could hear my unit chattering not fifty metres behind. Amongst the suck and surge of the current I thought I could hear a girl singing, a spritely voice, high and distant. At first I thought it was a patriotic song piped through the camp's loudspeakers - they often did this during long periods of inaction - but this was the voice of a daydreaming child. As I sat and listened I thought of the Tanabata tale, and my family setting off firecrackers by the river back home, eating watermelon and rice balls, writing wishes on wax paper and releasing them in the water. I hoped they wished for my safety. I looked up and saw exactly what they would see -Vega and Altair shining across the face of the galaxy.

A firework exploded. Red and white arcs fell. I hurried to finish. More explosions overhead. They were beautiful – Manchurian ones from over the border; expanding spheres of red and green with yellow tails. The drill had begun. Voices were shouting - my unit running back to their tunnels. I stood up and buckled my trousers.

The girl's voice was too pure and faltering for a piped record. I heard in the song the bird cries of lovers. Was there a lamp moving amongst the rocks? The voice seemed to be coming from under the bridge. I hoped the voice was Mei Li's. I knew I should hurry back to my unit but I was curious. My heart was steeped in the warm glow of our sexual union. I wanted the real woman again, not the crippled persona, cross-eyed and false. Perhaps, after the day's encounter, she now loved me and was calling me. I forgot her warnings. I stepped toward the bridge. The last thing I remember was a firework going off in my head, and I woke up on the stones with the sun rising in my eyes.

I felt numb, but at peace. My bootlaces were undone and my uniform disheveled. I climbed to my feet. The sun was sparkling on the river. The Marco Polo bridge marched across it; a monumental row of arches. The air was clean, the sunshine sharp, as if striking everything at a different angle. I studied everything closely and realised the telegraph wires across the bridge were gone. The airships above the bridge were gone. I knelt down and splashed my face in the clear water. There'd been a military exercise the night before, fireworks going off. I inspected myself for injury – bloodstains, burns – nothing but the nervous ache of my heartbeat. There were none of the usual sounds of an army camp – grinding truck engines, throbbing generators, instructions through loudspeakers. I looked for signs of my unit – no soldiers anywhere. Feeling like a lost child, I made for the bridge.

My boots crunched in the rubble. Flowers spangled along the path. It was a bright yellow day. I reached the road. Rice stretched emerald in every direction. Other fields were rich with crops of yellow and white flowers. The asphalt was gone. The radar towers were gone. Where there were barracks and grubby brown tents only kites flapped above the fields – mock birds of prey. Little bamboo windmills spun in the breeze. Buffaloes stood in lotus rich ponds. Workers bent in the fields under conical hats. Clusters of village rooves stood on the other side of the bridge. The lions still roared on the pillars lining the bridge but their eyes seemed wider and their teeth a little sharper. The village had the same rough topography but the buildings were shoddy and windowless. I kept looking around for my missing army.

A figure began to walk towards me across the bridge. I wasn't sure whether to run or call her for help. She carried a basket on her head but was not dressed like the market women who entered the camp; she wore a thick black robe, embroidered with plates of tin. Silver rings clasped her neck, as her face came into view, I saw she looked exactly like Mei Li. She had the same long nose, serpentine eyes, perfect symmetry of features.

I stammered her name involuntarily. She stopped and squinted at me with the same look as the day before, when she'd realised, "Ah. You are the boy that..." but today she said nothing. She looked me up and down with wide eyes, and I noticed half of her face was covered in a blue bruise.

"Mei Li? What happened?" I stepped toward her. Her lips quivered in fear. She stepped backwards and said something incomprehensible. The basket fell from her head. Various vegetables rolled across the wooden pylons. I held up my hands unthreateningly but with a jingle of jewelry she turned on her heel and ran back the way she had come, turning occasionally to see if I was chasing, her face a blue mask of horror.

I was starving so bent down and picked up a cucumber from the fallen basket. It tasted delicious. I ate several more and a sweet melon, which I smashed open on a pillar.

That was not Mei Li, I thought as I ate. This was the Marco Polo Bridge and my army garrison was not stationed beside it. How had the entire garrison moved? Had I been hit by a firework the night before? Was I concussed or imagining things? These were the best guesses I could make. I was certainly not capable of any clearer thought, because I sat there slurping on melon even while two horses cantered over the bridge towards me.

Both the horses and the guards on them were liberally protected with leather – masks, gloves, leggings. The riders wore copper helmets and breastplates, and wielded long iron lances which were pointed firmly at me. One stopped, the other circled around me and pointed his weapon at my back. I held up my arms in surrender, and felt strangely relieved, as if assistance had finally arrived.

The horses snorted and flicked their tails. The riders stared from their masks. Finally one rider shouted a gruff demand which I didn't understand, then repeated it. Then the other started shouting, gesturing at the spilled basket at my feet. I half-mimed in poor my mandarin that the girl had left it there and run away. My broken words seemed to stun the riders and they looked at each other, then one turned back and asked in a dialect I could barely discern, "where are you from?"

I thought for some time about my answer and finally told them that I was from an army based on the north side of the river. At this they laughed loudly. Then one waved the sharp tip of his lance menacingly close to my face, and used it to snag the strap of my combat helmet and flick it off. "Where is this army?" The other asked. My helmet clattered to the ground. The other swept it up and inspected it with some amazement. "I don't know." I grinned, no doubt sheepishly. My interrogators muttered exclamations. They each banged the steel dome, stretched the elastic strap, staring at me with great suspicion. Then they thrust their lances back at my chest and turned their horses. I was under arrest. The horsemen marched me across the Marco Polo Bridge into enemy territory.

To say I was bewildered is an understatement – my mind had simply given up. As we walked through the village, naked children crowded the doorways, silver-necked women pounded rice and barefoot men carried loads; all stopped to stare at me openmouthed. Most of the villagers were dressed in rags. All had black teeth. Some backed away, others pointed and yelled what sounded like curses. I suddenly realised I was a prisoner of war. In as many languages as I could recall, I demanded they uphold the articles of the Geneva Convention. The guards ignored me and led me to mud-brick oven with a rusty iron door. They threw me in with a dismissive yell, and carried my helmet away through the parting crowds. Children immediately clambered on the bars to make faces, further stifling the compartment of light and air, jeering and shouting. Then they began to spit. I retreated to the farthest wall, and discovered it already occupied by a portly man sitting on a stool. He was dressed in silk clothes that were dusty and torn.

"If you bring your legs up to this line, they can't hit you," he announced in something resembling French. "I have already measured it." Indeed there was a crude line scratched on the floor in charcoal. I tried to recall my schoolboy lessons. "They think you are a Vietnamese spy," he continued. "I think you are not. I just heard you speak several languages of the world, and more I didn't recognise. You are a well-educated man, and not of these parts." He turned to me, raised one bushy eyebrow, and shifted his stool to make room on the floor. My boots were already dripping with yellow sputum. I drew them behind the line. "The local witch doctors tell me there is a devil in their phlegm, but it's the flux I worry about," he pointed at some dry brown lumps on the floor. "Beasts." He handed me a small gourd.

"Drink a little. Not much," he offered. I sipped gratefully. It was almost raw alcohol.

"Where are we?" I managed to say.

"This is the village of Yongdao in the province of Xian, navel of the world. What kind of spy are you?" He smiled.

"I am not a spy." I announced. " I am a soldier with the Yamato Imperial Army, and I have had some kind of accident. Tell me," I whispered, fearing for my life, "what will these brigands do to us?"

"Us? They will shortly present me to the Emperor's envoy, who is on his way here as we speak. Then I'm sure this little misunderstanding will be sorted out." He growled. "As for you…" he shrugged. "If they continue to think you are a Vietnamese spy, they will kill you."

I was confused - The Xianese Royal line had been in exile since the September 18 Incident. Vietnam had been annexed by the Americans. I looked at the tiny cage we were in, and the yellow and green spittle on the floor. "Do these people recognise the Geneva Convention?"

He regarded me for some time incredulously. "What could you know of Geneva?" He enquired. "Geneva is a small crossroads in the Alps, with good pasture, I hear. I assure you its burghers hold no treaty with the viziers of the East!" He laughed again at the thought. He then squinted at me. "Who does your army fight for?"

"I serve the Emperor of the Shining Path, immortal liberator of the Mainland, champion of the provinces of Formosa and Manchuria." I intoned proudly.

The man's eyes narrowed. "I would watch what I say, young man. I assure you none of the Khan's maps contain any of the lands that you mention."

I laughed confidently. "My Emperor's maps do. My unit is, or was until last night, stationed on the other side of the Marco Polo Bridge." I pointed in that direction. A gob of spit landed on the back of my hand.

He snatched back his gourd. "Do not jest with me, donkey."

"Eh?" I asked.

"How do you know my name?"

"I don't know your name!" I protested.

"Were you sent here to interrogate me?" He shifted away from me.

"Interrogate you? I don't even know who you are!"

His eyes narrowed again. "Then you just confused me with a bridge."

"A bridge?" I laughed. "It has been named after Marco Polo since he visited this region centuries ago!" I smiled.

His brow furrowed. "I see that you are simpleton," he remarked, and withdrew further into the corner. I looked at his once fine silk coat, his gourd and his cracked leather shoes, and concluded it was he who was the outcast. A tramp, a drunkard, penniless.

I looked past the children hanging on the bars, most of whom had tired of spitting at us, and now made strange animal noises, imitating our foreign words. I looked at the windowless buildings and the bony people walking past, the mud walls and the clean blue sky. There was nothing in the village that wasn't made of wood, mud, water, or stone. Loin-clothed men in straw shoes carried bundles of wood. Goats chased chickens. There were no shops, no radios, no windows, wires or water pipes. The only familiar thing was the sky, free and empty. I longed for my quarters, my companions. Where were they?

It was stiflingly hot in the cell. The incidents of the previous day were vivid in my mind - I had uncovered a spy ring, lost my virginity, been knocked out in a military exercise, and taken prisoner by an unknown enemy. I felt bewildered and lost. I choked back tears, and fingered my army tags, perhaps my only hope of safety. The sharp ache in my chest returned. I unbuttoned my khaki tunic and gazed down at it with creeping horror – there was a wound there, a circle of sealed flesh around my heart. There had been no injury there the day before. Whatsmore this was a serious wound, its red scar still oozing fluids, an injury I had no recollection of at all. Whatsmore, it was no combat wound: it was an incision deliberately made. Hyperventilating, I shook the man next to me and, not sure how to phrase the question:"Sir, please take a look at my chest. What do you see there?"

He glared at me impatiently. "I see the carcass of a fool."

I annoyed him again. "Please Sir! Am I wounded?"

He sighed and glanced briefly down. "I see a thorax marked not by the blade of a clumsy barber.

Or is it the ritual cut of a savage tribe? Perhaps they swapped your heart with your brain, and tangled up your soul." Then he fell silent and avoided my eyes. Barbers? Swords? Tribes? I felt the loss of myself – my body, my bearings, my memories – and indeed felt tangled up. I began to imagine the impossible.

" Sir," I pestered him again. "Tell me what day it is today."

He shrugged off my hand, his eyes closed, as if asleep, or drunk.. "Ask these children."

"What day is it?!" I shouted at the children making faces at the bars. They giggled and swung. I repeated my demand, and one replied, as the others resumed their spitting, "the day of water!"

"And the year?"

"The year of the mouse!" This was very funny to them. "So it is," I nodded, calculating. "But what is, um, the year in numbers?" A gob of yellow spit landed on my trousers, and I pulled my legs back over the line. "It's the twelfth year of the Emperor… " I mumbled, and using my fingers translated this into the international calendar.

"Nineteen thirty seven!" I shouted. The man opened his eyes again and regarded me tiresomely from the corner.

"In my travels," he began, "I have found as many different ways of counting the years as there are languages to speak of it. In this country, it is the ninth year of the Yuan dynasty…" he sat up and became more authoritive, "but obviously your emperor counts differently. Time in the lands of Mohammedans is only four hundred years old, they say, while in countries in India they count in tens of thousands, based on the lifespan of their gods. But I have not heard that number you mention. What does it measure?"

I searched my schoolbook memories: "Anno domini!" I shouted. "1937 anno domini!"

Again Marco Polo's features again darkened. "A simpleton," he concluded to himself, then turned to me. "You poor fellow. You may have learned the name of the calendar of Europe, but not its count. It is 1285, give or take a year." He smiled at me as if I were a child. "Beware!" He wagged his finger. "Calendars are like labyrinths. You can't help but get lost." He picked up my tag, looked at the number engraved on it, then dropped it.

I didn't feel like a child, or a soldier, or even a sane person, sitting in the cage with him. "Yes," he said sympathetically, "you've got yourself thoroughly lost, haven't you?" He peered solemnly into my eyes. All his earlier rancor was gone. "To confess, I have too," he added sternly. "If there's one thing I have learnt on my travels, it is that I have got myself terribly, terribly lost." He sat up on his stool and held his finger in the air. "Not only that, but I always was, and always will be. Let me tell you, it takes an expert on maps – and calendars – to understand that." He laughed. "What to expect when every emperor and warlord turns the year back to zero when they assume command? Even the lord Jesus did that. So don't be afraid – 1285 is as good as anywhere to stop and get your bearings." He swept his arms around the airless box we were held in. "A good journeyman," he exclaimed, "is not a student of maps and measures but of stories. The tales he encounters on the way are his best source of knowledge, and these tales always say that a prison, for example, is as good as a palace, or that fools can be wise, and generally nothing is what it appears to be." He turned suddenly to me. "A well-told tale is a healthy draught from an ancient cellar – the storehouse of the soul. That storehouse is where the dead and the living dwell together. So take a drink and tell me a tale, my fool, for we both may soon be dead."

He held out his gourd again, and I stared at him dumbfounded. He waited for me to act, and then sighed. "No? Perhaps you are not as foolish as I think. Good tales come only from wise men or fools, you see, the only people who wish to know what the dead think. Some stories last forever," he shrugged, "and some die still-born. So, while we wait to be taken to the Emperor's palace, or in your case to his dungeons, let me tell you a story from these parts. It is a very childish and ancient one." He looked to me for approval.

"Go ahead," I replied, and he began.

The Origin of the Years

"Many people ask what is the origin of the years? Why do the years in which we are born take the characters of animals, and how do they influence the character of man? Well, a long time ago, the universe was much smaller than it is today, so there was less time, and the days were much slower. Since time was slower, matter was lighter. And since the stars were lighter and purer, so were the souls of living things: there hadn't been enough time to build up the heavy momentum of right and wrong, cause and effect, that we have today. So this meant that Emperors were far more divine, being less encumbered by the weight of their subjects' actions, for which all Emperors must answer at the gates of heaven. Anyway, one day - which itself had lasted for as long as living memory - the Emperor saw that the sun was becoming old for the very first time. It had begun to sink down the sky, and he watched it struggle back up, then fall a bit lower again, steamy and cool, until obviously it couldn't rise any further.

"The Emperor, who had tended the crops and the weather, and the waters and the soil, saw now his crops were dying, and the winds were becoming icy, not warm and sweet, and the rivers and oceans were freezing over, and his subjects – the animals and people - fell into despair. "Where are the flowers?" They called. "Where is our bread, and fruit and wine? Call yourself an Emperor? Do you not have power over these things?"

Of course the Emperor did, but he did not have power over time. He saw there was nothing he could do to stop the death of the sun, but he also saw, in his divine and cruel wisdom, how to create a new one.

"He organised a great feast, and invited all the animals to attend. "It will be held in honour of the sun," he declared, "who will be the guest of honour. All will be able to bask in its warmth, and feast to the brim on its harvest: fruits and grain, cheeses and breads, honeys and pastries."

"The Emperor understood that all creatures were ruled as much by their appetites as they were by him, so he expected them all to race to be first to the occasion, and so sit closest to the sun, and have the choicest pickings at the expense of the others. He was right, and all the animals devised their strategy, according to their natures. The tiger simply assumed she would be given a royal welcome, and a seat near the table's head, so she did not fret, and lay in the long grass to sleep, as is her habit. The horse, being the fastest of all the animals, knew the race was his, and munched away on the last of the sweet clovers, in preparation for his spectacular gallop to the finish line. The monkey knew it didn't matter whether he was first or last, because he would simply sneak and trick and snatch his way to the best seats and meats, so he continued to play in the trees and annoy all the other animals. And so on – all the animals naturally assumed they were the cleverest and most honoured, important guest and would get to the top of the table first: the dragon planned to smash his way into the feasting hall, the dog would sniff out a shortcut, the chicken saw itself soaring high through the air above the others, and the boar could eat more and faster than the rest, so he considered the feast itself, not the trip there, as the race to win.

"Only one animal took on the task with anything resembling humbleness and practicality – the cow. The cow realised he was the slowest and dumbest of the animals, and set off well before the feast, at a steady pace, with a good map and full stomachs. One other animal was equally as organised as the cow – the mouse. She got up a bit later, washed her face, put on her best trousers, packed a hamper and followed the cow's muddy hoof-prints. Soon she spied the cow on the road ahead, and scurried up towards it.

"All the other animals left it to the last minute to rouse themselves and leave for the Emperor's palace. But before the last minute came, something terrible happened: the sun set. It had spent its last day crawling along the horizon on its knees – suddenly it fell. It could barely drag itself to the Emperor's palace, where the servants took it in, and put it in its place at the head of the table, where it wheezed and drowsed, barely alive. All the animals were left to find their way in the dark.

"The cow had a map, and was well over half way there, so he was OK. The mouse grew tired, and ran up the cow's tail, as it had planned along, and spent the rest of the journey resting silently in the furry hair between the cow's horns. The other animals fanned out across the countryside, lost and hopeless, falling down ditches and looking for bridges and signposts, crying out for the sun. The tiger set off last, confused by the long night but still certain she would win, as she was the only animal who could see in the dark. She raced past the other animals, seeing clearly ahead through the moonless countryside, until she saw the golden palace shining gloriously in the distance – and, to her horror, approaching its wide-open gates at a tired bovine plod, was the cow! The tiger roared and ran at full speed – the cow, terrified, hearing the tiger bounding up behind him snarling, stopped in its tracks at threshold of the palace.

"Whereupon the mouse, seeing its chance, leapt from between the cow's horns and scampered through the gates.

"Trumpeters appeared to herald the event. Flags and banners unfurled from the palace towers. The Emperor himself opened the huge doors. The mouse had won!

" 'Congratulations, little mouse! You have proven yourself, amongst all the animals, to be the most versatile, cunning and strong, to have used all the gifts of life, mind and body to the greatest advantage,' praised the Emperor. 'Welcome to the feast at the end of the first year, where you will take first place beside your maker the sun, and from henceforth through eternity, this year will be known as the Year of the Mouse!'

"With a little poke of her tongue at the tiring cow and the cowering tiger, the mouse cheered and ran inside the palace. The Emperor closed the doors on the runners-up, and bid them wait.

"The mouse ran through the corridors to a great banquet room filled with tables decked with the choicest offerings from the earth: the sweetest corn, the fattest grains, the tastiest roots, the most aromatic herbs, the juiciest fruit and the most colourful wine. It was all there, bending the tables, as high as a hill and as wide as a field, and the mouse was overcome with sensation.

" 'Where can I start? Where can I sit?' Squealed the mouse.

"The emperor looked around. 'Oh, er, you won't need a chair,' he said uncertainly, having forgotten that detail. 'You can just, um, dive in wherever you like. Don't mind your manners, just because of me.'

" 'You mean it's just me? All for me?' Squeaked the mouse, and it leapt from table to table, devouring succulent grapes, bouncing on giant loaves and swimming in lakes of cream, until she saw, seated in a giant throne at the far end of the room, a charcoal ball, a respiring cinder - the ancient sun. But this sun wasn't glorious and golden – it was sagged and burnt and black. It looked like old char in a neglected fireplace, with barely a lick of flame keeping it alive.

" 'Come on sun!' Chipped the sated mouse, smeared in food, 'its been a glorious year! A wonderful year – the year of me! Join the feast!'

"The sun sleepily opened one eye, and with a smoky gasp, managed to reply: 'Ah, a mouse,' he closed his eye, and wearily opened it again, 'the champion of animals. Indeed you've had a good year, and we have laboured long together. Look around you, the harvest is huge, and all things have grown to their peak. But all things emerge from me, and as I rise and pass, so do you, dear mouse. It is time to meet your maker.' And with that, the sun picked the rodent up by the tail, and popped it quickly in its charred mouth. "There was some coughing, and sticking of bones, and a little trouble swallowing, for the mouse was the first thing the sun had ever eaten, but eventually the creature was devoured, and the sun drifted off to sleep again, after emitting a steamy light-filled belch.

"The Emperor flung open the gilded palace doors again. 'While not as clever or quite as nimble as the mouse,' he said with a mixture of condescension and glee, "the cow is next. Dear servant, you performed with great dedication and purpose of mind, and an admirable sense of your own shortcomings. You are thoroughly deserving - more deserving than the tiger…' The Emperor glared down at the furious feline on the palace steps with such severe majesty that it stopped its growling and kowtowed at the ruler's feet. '…of runner up amongst the animals, and to have the coming second year eternally named: the Cow!'

"As a last gesture before entering, the cow raised its tail, and with a teasing moo, dropped a steaming pile of green turds on the tiger's head. It then sauntered inside. The tiger could do nothing but maintain his poo-smeared posture at the feet of the Emperor, who laughed and closed the door again.

" 'Where's my food," the cow mooed as it was led through the jeweled halls of the palace. "What a full room!" He drooled at the extent of the fodder that was spread across the banquet hall. "Are there any rules?" He mooed again and looked around, "and where's that fool the mouse?'

" 'First things first,' the Emperor cleared his throat. 'We thought you wouldn't need a stool. You can graze freely wherever you wish. The sun is er, reclined at the other end of the room, waiting to meet you, and the mouse is er, sleeping it off upstairs. You can meet her there shortly. Enjoy your meal!'

"The cow was already munching through a bowl of honeyed oats and raisins, and then moved onto a pile of asparagus and cabbage… with tail swishing and both stomachs gurgling, it chewed its way through the hall, until it saw the sun waking and stretching in its chair.

" 'How are you sun," called the cow, and even half-bowed before the drowsy orb. 'You look more like the moon,' he snickered stupidly. In fact the sun was feeling much better. The black flakes had fallen from its burnt-out skin, and a faint creamy light had replaced the smoky gasps of only a few moments before. But it didn't let on to the cow how much better it felt.

" 'Oh,' he groaned. 'It's been such a long, long year, but with the help of all my animal friends I'll soon be back in sorts. Now brown cow,' he gazed the muscled beast up and down, 'what a fine creature you are. I want to thank you for all your hard work over the last year in making this harvest so appealing. But I have one last job to ask of you.'

" 'Certainly, esteemed one. I will do whatever you ask.'

" 'Can you carry me on your strong back to the rest room?'

" 'It will be an honour,' replied the cow, and knelt down dutifully. Using the last of the strength it had metabolized from the mouse, the sun stood up on shaky, burnt legs, managed to get one over the cow's shoulder, and commanded it to stand. Then the sun drew a carving knife from its shadowy beams and slit the beast's throat from ear to ear. As the cow fell to the tiles, the sun held a golden cup to the gush of blood, and raising it high before the cow's startled stare, toasted: 'The coming year is yours, dear cow. You are its herald, and unforgotten friend.' He drank the cow dry. He then picked up the carcass and dispatched it, limb by limb, growing brighter and brighter with each swallow. Then the sun again sat back in its throne and nodded off to sleep.

"The Emperor kicked the cow's four hooves into the kitchen and went to summon the tiger. There's no need to describe the fate of the jealous and hubristic cat, or the remainder of the bewildered beasts, who trickled slowly in from the long night outside the palace, in the order we know today - an order set by their natural inclinations, talents and flaws. Such is destiny. They all attended their final feast alone, ignorant of the ultimate truth of their existence, glimpsing with their fading sense the full brilliance of the Emperor's plan. All fell back into the bottomless belly of the sun, who after three days of feasting and sleeping rose shining from the palace into the sky, as bright and yellow and as hot as it had been on the first day of creation.

"The Emperor rejoiced, and so did all the people of the world, who knelt down before him, and declared themselves saved. They planted new crops, and bred new animals to eat in the great circle of life, and every subsequent year as the sun grew dark and old, the people prepared a great feast, and the animals were led back into the sun in the order set down for all time."

*   *   *

Marco Polo stopped talking, and held his gourd to his lips. "What do you think of that?" He asked, as if we had just eaten an unexpected dish. I sat thinking for some time, then carefully replied, "I've never heard anything like it. It sounds cobbled together from half a dozen children's stories and legends, to be honest."

"I agree." He shrugged impartially. "It is too complex to be truly satisfying. But it has a colourful plot, which blends both fabulous and moral elements, yet…" he made a puzzled expression. "It is internally inconsistent. For example, if the sun ate all the animals, how did they return?"

"Yes. It raises more questions than it answers," I agreed, "and the attempt to link the character and destiny of man at the beginning seemed digressive.

Which raises an unanswered question – where is man in the tale?" I added.

Marco Polo stared at me in wide-eyed query. "You mean man the animal? Good question! Why were the animals devoured by the sun, but not the people? This is the story's major inconsistency. Where is the Year of Man?"

"Well…" I conjectured, "perhaps the Year of Man is yet to come."

He froze in mid-thought. "Yes, yes, good idea! A sequel. Now that is worth considering." He pulled a stub of charcoal from his coat, and made a mark on a worn piece of parchment covered in odd shapes. "A mnemonic code," he explained, "to mark our place in the labyrinth."

At that point there was a sharp click as our cage was unlocked. A guard beckoned from outside and the naked children ran off. Marco Polo stood and collected his bag. "Well, my new friend," he shuffled to the door, "it seems our allotted time together is over." He held up his bound hands for the guard drag him out. "As coincidence has it, I'm off to meet the Emperor." He bent through the open door and grinned reassuringly. "As I said, from the prison to the palace, nothing is what it seems." A bullock cart was waiting outside, which the guards helped him climb into. "Good luck! Don't get any more lost!" He waved as best he could as the cart lurched away, and they were gone.

The gate hung open. No-one was guarding it. The village was almost empty. I expected the mounted soldiers who had brought me here to run up, but a minute passed. I poked my head out. I saw the bullock cart disappear around a corner in the distance. "Hello?" I shouted. One or two passers-by glanced briefly at me and continued, with none of the fear or curiosity that was there before. Was I free? I quickly stepped outside and stood up, and walked casually away from the cell. No-one came. Perhaps it was some kind of siesta. I saw women sleeping in the hallways of their hovels, men dozing in distant squares. I walked further away from the cell. Nothing. There was the sound of a pipe playing somewhere. I turned and strode quickly toward the bridge. When I rounded the last corner I skidded to a halt.

Rolls of barbed wire surrounded the approaches to the bridge. Loudspeakers crackled patriotic songs. Grey airships hovered over the rows of brown tents. Diesel engines ground along the tracks. All was back to normal. Two Kuomintang guards on the bridge shouted at me, white-faced, raising their guns, and for the second time in a day I dutifully surrendered.

Their commanding officer looked at my tag number and, with an air of panic, immediately picked up the telephone. I heard him ask for Yamamoto, say my name, then they hurried me across the bridge. When I got back to our checkpoint, telephones were ringing and senior officers were sprinting up to the guard-house.

I trembled in my boots, which were still marked with the village children's sputum. I was taken to a room where Yamamoto demanded to know where I'd been. I told him a mixture of what I could remember and what would make sense – I'd wandered to the river's edge the night before, and when the fireworks began everything went black. I'd woken up the next day on the opposite bank of the river, and wandered into the Kuomintang village.

How had I got to the opposite side? He demanded. I said I didn't know. Had the Kuomintang kidnapped me? I said no. I didn't tell him about the cell or Marco Polo. I supposed it had been a strange vivid dream, brought on by concussion. Had I heard shots around the bridge where I'd disappeared? I assured him no. Several empty Kalishnikov rounds had been found under the bridge, along with… the stenographers and junior officers went silent as he drew from a bag two broken and blackened bits of metal - the remains of his sword. He held the handle up, his face red with rage. Did I know anything of that? His bottom lip was trembling. No I did not, I assured him, equally speechless with shock, because I'd last seen that sword in the hands of Mei Li.

I was taken outside to a wire holding pen. Events and tempers had obviously spiraled out of control in my absence: inside were three bound and captured KMT soldiers. One of them was Hei Jin. His face was bruised and swollen but he was staring at me in awestruck fear. His finger slowly lifted to my face, shaking. "He's alive!"

Crowing, Yamamoto asked - was this the soldier they had kidnapped? Another captive, a sergeant, looked at me and shook his head. There had been no kidnapping, he replied. There were reports of gunfire from under the bridge during the military exercise.

Communist insurgents had been seen in the area. Yamamoto ordered Hei Jin removed from the pen. He was kicked onto his chest and knees. Then why does he recognise him, Yamamoto demanded. Hei Jin said nothing and his arm was broken behind his back. The KMT sergeant calmly interrupted, promising an independent investigation of my disappearance and the shooting. KMT agents had also stolen and destroyed important cultural properties, Yamamoto yelled, brandishing pieces of his sword. Sobbing and kowtowing before the enemy, Hei Jin said he only knew me from the handball games.

In a terrible fury, Yamamoto threw down his broken heirloom. He marched to a colleague and asked to borrow his sword. Then with a single practiced dance he beheaded his captive. Hei Jin's body pitched forward like a sack, spraying blood. The head rolled forward in the dirt, gasping. The legs kicked as the body squirted itself dry. Hei Jin was meeting his maker, alone, perhaps glimpsing his place in history.

No-one said anything. Yamamoto stood calmly, walked to the telephone and delivered a momentous series of orders. Then he returned and dragged the sergeant and third soldier into the open square, and beheaded them as well. As his artillery bombardment of the Kuomintang village began, starting a war that has, in some places, yet to end, he and two other officers carried out on their victims the traditional warrior class' punishment of criminals: overcome with offence and indoctrinated with national pride, they reduced the flesh and bones of their executed prisoners to smaller and smaller sections, testing the mettle of their beloved swords. When they were finished, Yamamoto ordered his dogs into the square, and his tanks across the Marco Polo Bridge. So history changed course on a whim, a burst of rage, a hubristic moment of pride.

As I manned by position and watched the tracer bullets and mortars fly, the voice began again – the same eerie song I'd heard the night before under the bridge, but now I understood it was for my ears only, or rather, it came from my heart, tugging at the strange scars that had appeared there. High and pure, the voice seemed to raise me out of the gruesome material plane I was experiencing, into an alternate realm where peasant girls became fearsome lovers, bridges spanned not rivers but centuries, and the sun was a wild cosmic creature, cruel and hungry. Around me blew the fogs of war, ignorance and history, but inside a spirit was awakening, cleansing the defilements in my blood, blowing away the fog, stripping away the illusions of men and their mortality.

Now, looking back from my picnic chair under the bridge, the tracers that zipped between the river banks look just like fireflies bobbing between the trees, and the mortars bursting over the rooftops are fireworks in the hands of ignorant children, and the soldiers marching across the bridge look like lost souls rushing to a great feast, misunderstanding their own natures, waiting for the Year of Man.

Big Ears

One of my grandchildren has stopped and is staring up at me with round urgent eyes. I can't tell which one it is - they all seem whelped from the same litter to me, like fresh stamps of the mould.

"Why can't humans marry fairies grandpa?"

While she has been running around with sparklers and ice cream, this question has been turning over in her mind, and it now requires an authoritive answer.

"They should be able to," I declare, then whisper to her, "but something's gone wrong with the world." She bites her lip and stares at me,

"You see, once, everything was locked together as one," I hold up my walking cane and spin it into a blur, "but it soon broke into different speeds and scales and times. Down looks different from up," I hold it vertically, "and big differs from small. Here is never there," I whiz the cane behind her back, "and right always looks different from wrong. On one level things are hard, gross and solid, like people," I pinch her arm, " and on another they are airy, light and made of nothing, like fairies. Everything has been forced apart." Her eyes are wide open in alarm, but she nods with the simple understanding only a child can have.

"The important thing to remember is that all the opposites are just two ends of the same stick." I grin, pleased with my explanation. She stares back, suspiciously.

"Come on, it's wishing time!" A mother claps her hands. Everyone runs up. It's time to launch our Tanabata wishes. We have already made our boats: vessels of waxed paper and coloured sails, on which we have scrawled our demands – electric cars and computer games, success and love affairs, exam results and dog vests, magic wands and long vacations, babies and rocket ships, slimmer bodies and better friends, richer husbands, kinder wives, royal titles, bigger TVs. The human heart is forever incomplete; we launch them downstream. It's said that if a paper boat reaches the sea, the wish will come true. There they go, bobbing and tipping in a damp morass, fleeting desires indeed, tugging on our hearts; I can't help feel they are doomed, but more will take their place. The children set off the last of the fireworks: a crackling climax of sparks and sound.

The adults pack up the blankets and chairs and cooler boxes, but I want to sit here in my wobbly picnic chair and watch the rivers flow, the one above – the galaxy boiling in its dust lanes - and the one below. The traffic bridge is a shadow of that one above, a mould of concrete, littered by advertising. Down here, models float among golden wares, up there Altair and Vega are gazing hungrily at each other, and I know the bridge between them will soon be complete. The loudspeakers cackle into life: "This family facility is closing," a maternal voice laments. "It's time for everyone to go home. Don't forget to update your location status as you leave. Goodnight." Sleepy muzac plays.

There is movement up there – wings fluttering through vast space. Avian wings to ferry a farmer to his fairy-bride? No: thick steel bodies are moving above the clouds. Black ships are crossing the city, blotting out chunks of sky, scrambling radar frequencies. Imperial City is under guard tonight.

The shapes swooping overhead are drones heading to the Occupied Zones. They will bomb the houses of Northern commanders, who have been renewing their threats to launch long-range missiles. A million soldiers are amassed on our borders. They send sleepwalkers into our subways and shopping malls. The airborne flotilla becomes a throb of engines, drowning out the rush of the river and the piped muzac.

My grown children, dressed in their Big Ears t-shirts and plastic slippers, discuss the TV gossip programmes as if nothing has happened. Don't they notice the tonnes of military hardware that just passed over their heads? They are doctors and civil servants and office staff – mature people occupying essential positions in society. They believe themselves free, but they are in thrall to the system around them. Its distracting frisson blocks their eyes and ears. I am a silly, frail old man, as ridiculously dressed as they. The planes overhead are triggering my memories and fantasies again; a fairy amongst the cement arches, singing in a wild voice; my post-traumatic stress, dementia, call it what you will. They believe I am at their mercy – or at least in thrall to their constant care – but I am nothing of the sort. Tonight, I am at the mercy of the ages.

Thoughts are being twisted out of my brain like the stars wheeling. I feel the universe squeezing itself through this corpuscular flesh, wringing out what it can; soon it will drop my sorry carcass and re-assemble itself elsewhere.

"Upsy-daisies grandpa," a son-in-law smiles indulgently at me. "I'll walk you to the car."

They want to drive me through the hard stinking streets to their flimsy boxes in the suburbs, but I will have none of it, and wave them away. One of my daughters sighs. "He's always like this at Tanabata. He wants to mope about indulging his memories of the war. Last year he refused to come on the picnic, and this year he refuses to leave. Oh well…" she looks at me with genuine pity.

"I'm staying here! I have an appointment with the Emperor!" I remind her.

"You can call him from home!" She shouts back, exasperated. As if re-asserting itself after the flotilla, a repellant, ear-splitting tune blares from the loudspeakers. "This facility is closed!" The voice insistently reminds us. "Please exit."

"He won't answer," I reply, ignoring the din. "He is stuck in his palace, watching celebrity chat shows." They laugh. "The Emperor is just like everyone else," I opine, "except he has a bigger flat-screen." I stand up and hand someone my chair. "Thankyou. I've had a wonderful time with your children, and now I shall walk home."

They look at me aghast. "Don't be silly! You'll never make it. The police will stop you. You'll catch a chill."

"I'm wearing my tails." I show them.

"But you can't wander around the city in those!"

"Why not?" I raise my top hat in fun.

"Because you'll get beaten up by a motorcycle gang."

They're right – teenagers on scooters roam the city at night, looking for old men to beat up. They steal their wallets and pee on their faces. The police can't seem to stop them, though some say that's because the children are their own. I suspect that the police are just like everyone else: too occupied to do anything properly. They have to monitor crowds, update their status, keep track of the ticker on their desks. I wield my cane. "A-ha! They are no match for an old soldier like me!" I growl and swish at the children, who sprint, terrified, towards the family fleet.

The sensible daughter glares at me. "Come on then, if he wants to risk his neck, let him. He'll be back home before we know it, asking for his glass of milk and hot water bottle." I can tell she thinks I want to visit the snack bars nearby, to drink whisky and fondle the hostesses. She's right. I smile as the rest of the tribe meekly follow her to the cars.

The loudspeakers repeat their message. The scheduled outdoors period is over. Soon the Safety Teams will patrol the streets.

"Big Ears!" One of the children squeals, and we all look up. The blunt nose of an airship floats above a nearby apartment block, barely clearing building height. On one side is stenciled monumentally the unmistakeable form of Big Ears: two oval black ears and a parabola-dish nose. On the other side a flat-screen advertises a Giants vs Tigers game in zany gold-red graphics. A slogan pops up:

They Are What They Are
I am What I Am: Happy!

"Big Ears!" The families cheer, and I smile and wave too in happy recognition. The airship floats slowly above the bridge, sucking up our cell-phone chats and status updates. Airbrushed snaps of this season's fast food decorate the screen. Deep-fried octopus drenched in gravy. Grilled eel and golden turkey. The motivational message switches over:

Live For Today
Work For Tomorrow

Re-assured and looking forward to the game, the family sparks the engines of their satellite-navigated cars and drives sensibly home. I fix a toothless wet smile on my face and creep towards the Golden Lion Snack Bar.

The Golden Lion Snack Bar

She lifts her hair and looks askance at her image, while sliding the kanzashi-comb through her silver-black coils. The roots of her hair tighten as the comb grips. She lets go and a stray coil falls past her face. Perfect. The top of the comb is softly curved turtle-shell laquer, inlaid with mother of pearl - a chrysanthemum design. It doesn't stick out like a spade handle – it hides in the bun of her hair and flashes. Is it antique or retro-new? She doesn't know much about such things – she will have to ask Ambrose. She bends this way and that to check her new kimono's fit. Both gifts were waiting for her in the dressing room, the kimono still wrapped in its shop plastic. It is a traditional summer design: white clouds over kingfisher blue. She bows to the mirror and makes sure she can glimpse her shoulders beyond the stiffened collar, the powdered flesh gradually fading to shadow. Kimonos are simultaneously chaste and seductive: enclosing a woman's body yet eroticising her neck, and hence her face.

She is uncomfortably aware that these are not just gifts. It's been a long time since she felt she was wearing a kimono out of choice. She used to, and it delighted her as much as her clients. It all started with the chat-show hosts after the first wave of sleepwalker attacks. Their new designs were daring and deeply political at the time, defiant amongst the subway rubble and awe. The threats to the homeland created a nostalgic nationalism and the fashion spread to hostesses and shop assistants, who made it austere and chic. No more of the frilly foreign dresses or trivial casualness of the past. The atmosphere of the country changed. Flags were hung everywhere, patriotic songs played in the shopping malls. Her businessman clients started to wear the robes of the old clans. She lacquered her hair and chalked her face in the traditional style. Her clients found it cheerful and positive. It was time to take our country back, they said. Time to stop being ashamed of the War and the occupation, to deal with the aberrant Northern regime.

Now she finds expensive new accessories in her dressing room when she arrives, courtesy of this client or that company. Even minor clients like Ambrose feel obliged to keep up. Oh well, it is only a kimono, she thinks, as she opens her phone and updates her status. She only has to put it on, not take it off. *Bean's booked a private room ...>_<...3hrs of fake smiles coming up!* She snaps her phone closed, kneels, and opens the sliding paper doors.

There he is, the shrunken little man, sitting at a low table in the middle of the room.

"Good evening! I was hoping you would come tonight!" She cries happily. She notices he is wearing extremely formal dress – tails and a bow tie - like at state reception or a wedding. She knows Ambrose has a client crush on her, the gifts proved it, but tails? Her heart drops. Tonight is probably some major anniversary: his wife's death perhaps, or the cherry.

"Lovely to see you, Saori. You look wonderful."
His face creases into a smile. He has missing teeth,
his cheeks are wrinkled and yellow. Bean – her
secret nickname for him – gets better every time.

"Thankyou," she slides on her knees to the broad
table and places cold tea and snacks before him.
"The kimono is exquisite. I am not worthy of it."

"No, it suits your complexion which has the
paleness of summer clouds."

She straightens her back and smiles, even though
his clumsy compliment makes her blanch. She
doesn't like him thinking of her skin. "And the
comb? Does it match?" She pouts, moving her head
this way and that.

"Yes. Its perfect, if I do say so myself."

"It looks antique. Is it? You know more about such
things than me." Her eyes glow as she looks up at
him. She has completely adopted her projected role
– to complement her clients' self-image. This is
what his gifts have bought.

"It's from the war period," he says. "It belonged to
my sister."

She is taken aback. "A family heirloom? I
can't…."

"It's been sitting in a drawer for years. We lost her
in the partition."

"I am so sorry, Ambrose." She bows her head to
hide her narrowing eyes. He has given her the
possession of a dead woman.

"When I returned from the war," he continues,
"everything my family owned was destroyed. We
had relatives in the north, and my sister had been

sent there. She may still be there now, or… not. Like so many, she just disappeared. But that was sixty years ago. The comb should no longer lie in the dark. It should be worn by a woman as beautiful as you."

You poor man," she says, blinking eyes full of tears, wanting to tear the comb out of her hair. "Excuse my ignorance. I don't know much about the war." She wipes the table unnecessarily, She wants to start the usual games: banter, drink, teasing. She reaches out and touches his lapel, eyeing him up and down elaborately. "So what is the occasion Ambrose? You are dressed like the Emperor."

"Tanabata." He announces. She frowns. Tanabata is the most frivolous of the seasonal festivals. It's a shallow fairytale, appealing only to children, and further evidence that Bean is losing his marbles.

"Surely you don't dress up for Tanabata," she scolds, "other than to entertain your grandchildren?"

"Oh, of course," he waves, "but I have an additional appointment tonight." His eyes have a faraway look – uh-oh, she thinks, here comes the memory – the cherry, or the long-dead wife, or the comrade lost in the war. These phantoms make her job so much more difficult. She has to not just play nymph to his fantasies, but nursemaid to his memories.

"Additional to me?" She flirts. "A man… or a woman?"

"With the Emperor." He says matter-of-factly, and sips his tea.

She giggles. "I see…" She wipes the table again, flashing her neck and shoulders, A further sign of dementia. It will be a long three hours.

"Let me strengthen you for your auspicious meeting," she comments, " whisky, or wine?"

But he is staring at the webscreen above her, which is showing animated parabolas - the projected trajectories of the rocket tests threatened by the North.

"It's the same war," he nods up.

"We shouldn't be tolerating this," she recites, "Whisky or wine?" He orders whisky and she bows deeply at the door, closes it, stands up on the rock step, opens her phone and checks her mail. There is a string of replies. She thumbs *he's wearing tails, would you believe? For a meeting with the emperor!* /^_^\, then sets off down the path to visit her other clients.

The snack bar is designed like a garden, with lamps spotlighting various features: a pond, curiously-shaped rocks, a ceramic pot containing lotus. Stone pathways lead to private rooms. The finance company group in the Willow Room are playing a unity game. Their digital batons rise and fall in a synchronised patterns, while their online avatars squeak and cheer on the screen. The workers faces are turning in unison, speechless. She replaces their glasses of tea and moves on. She can feel Ambrose's dead sister's comb gripping her hair like a claw. She can't wait to remove it.

Tobacco smoke billows out of the Red Pine Room. She kneels in the doorway. The plastics company group are gorging. The table is piled with a half-eaten banquet. Two senior officials are sleeping on the table, mouths open. One man is kneeling in the corner, vomiting in the basin provided. Others are toasting each other, eyes squeezed closed. She begins smiling, pouring drinks. The group are discussing politics, deals, factions. One webscreen is tuned to soft porn, the other to news. They are surrounded in lingerie, politicians, lipstick, hot sighs, riot footage from the Occupied Zone. One woman is kneeling in a semi-formal pose, swaying gently, drunk, as a man gropes inside her white office shirt. The old men are talking about victory over the North, freeing the slaves from the factories. The vomiter returns to the table to wild applause. The woman pulls her coworker up from the table; clutches him, staggering, dancing to nothing. The leadership is suicidal and corrupt, the old men say, driven mad by hubristic fantasies. They drink planeloads of French champagne while the populace eat weeds. They run international drug and arms operations, casinos; they are a criminal gang. The workers stumble and fall onto the table with a crash. Saori apologises and scampers around them while they giggle uncontrollably. She bows promises to come back with more towels.

At the bar a bearded young man orders a bucket of Cool Sweat. His eyes are flicking strangely as he stares at his phone. On the screens above the counter people are evacuating a subway station. Then the parabolas arch out from the Northern launch sites again. As she fills the bucket she thinks about the recent rallies around the Great Leader, and a cold fear rises in her chest. Northern sleeper agents are controlled by coded transmissions to handheld devices. The customer at the bar is sweating and grimacing as he thumbs his keyboard furiously.

"How are the Giants?" She shouts as she serves the man his bucket, but he ignores her. On the screen the Defence Minister is giving a news conference. "Please continue your regular lives during the hours the North has announced it will conduct the tests." The bar goes silent but the man keeps playing his game. "The government will notify the public immediately the launches take place, so please stay alert." The bearded man's face is puffed in concentration as he reads something on his device. There's a sports update: the Giants are 8-6 down. She frowns and returns to the plastics group.

She looks at them The fallen couple are still rolling on the floor, covered in food. Someone else is vomiting, someone else sleeping. She wipes the table, turns down the sound, places clean towels beside them and shuffles out to collect Ambrose's bottle and there's a scream - the young man at the bar throws his phone at the floor and walks out, kicking the door as he leaves. Heart-beating, she bells the security guards, then collects the shattered device and puts it behind the counter. She feels a panic attack coming on and updates her status.

Weirdo smashing things up <@@>

Kovacs replies immediately.

It's the launches. Some citizens can't hold their nerve.

She thumbs back a smile. Security reports: *Got him*.

She feels better, but she's got a dead woman's claw in her hair. She collects Ambrose's order from the kitchen. The boat-shaped bowl holds a glistening square of tofu. The pearly white flesh is stained with soya sauce and topped with ginger. She places his chopsticks on a ceramic stand and pours him a straight whisky.

"Silk finger tofu." She announces.

"Made from seawater." He slices a delicate wall of flesh and slips it in his mouth. "A dish this kitchen has served for how many hundred years?"

About as old as you, she thinks. Doesn't he know how ridiculous he looks? His tails are threadbare and faded - an old suit he's kept since his youth. "Your jacket is making the room feel hot." She jokes.

"Of course, "he laughs fakely. "But if I take it off I will look like a common office worker next to you, so I must bear the weight of my generosity."

He doesn't look like an office worker, she thinks, he looks exactly like what he is – a geriatric who is waited on by his daughters. "You could never look common Ambrose."

He laughs again. "I last wore this suit at my granddaughter's wedding, and before that at my daughter's, and before that when I last met the Emperor, fifty odd years ago."

"Yes. The teahouse scroll. The national museum exhibition." She smiles: this is her profession - to be an expert on her clients' lives. She can instantly recall the personal histories and predilections of one hundred men, and each one thinks she knows them best. This is why they pay her. She could be a diplomat or a company director but she lives on tips.

"Your private reception with the Emperor. Whatever did you two talk about, Ambrose?"

"Football. Women. Television." He says. "Two typical men. He was pleasant enough, but he hadn't bothered to read the scroll."

She lowers her voice. "Ambrose, dear, why are you really dressed up tonight? I know it's not for another meeting with the Emperor…"

He pauses so long, balancing the slippery food on his sticks, making slow shaking attempts to get it into his mouth, that she wonders if he has heard her. He nearly finishes his plate before he looks up and grins at her shyly.

"As you know, at Tanabata, a bridge opens up across the river of stars so that forbidden lovers can make a tryst."

She feels tiny steps on her skin, a sensation she recognises with professional skill – the unwanted projection of male desire. It feels like seawater in her veins. Does he really think he can seduce her? She imagines herself grinding up and down on his octogenarian body. It would be an act of kindness – but impossible.

"Yes, it's a charming story," she says carefully. She hopes he will make an obvious pass at her, so she can reject it and end this pantomime.

"They spend only one night in each other's arms, before the gravity of the real world drags them apart," he adds. Her skin crawls and she faces the table, reddening. She realises she is acting coyly, so she forces her head up and looks him in the eyes.

"Such trysts belong in fairytales Ambrose. They can't exist in the real world, as you say."

He leans back against the wall behind him and stares at her for a long time, sipping his whisky. He is clutching his chest, as if there is pain there. Please, please don't have a coronary on my shift, she thinks. She bites her lip and reddens some more. "I'm sorry, I have destroyed the playful atmosphere."

"Not at all. The inappropriate allusion is my mistake. I am unskilled as a storyteller. Let me confess - I have dressed up today not because of the Emperor, or your allure, nor the vanity that serves it. I dress like a fool on Tanabata because it is the night I started the Patriotic War."

She ignores his insult and forces her burst of laughter into an empathic smile. These poor old soldiers. His skinny wrists shake as he grasps the bottle. "Let me," she says gently. Their fingers brush as the small glazed pot changes hands. She fills his cup and waits. Are his eyes rimmed in tears, or just an old man's blinking moistness? She can feel the years flowing and pushing away from him, tugging him from the present. He raises the full cup to his lips and the alcohol falls in puddles on the wooden tabletop. He puts it down without drinking and stares at the garden sadly. He has ceased to be annoying and again becomes an ancient man tossed by the tides of his memories. The blotched skin on his face is tight around the cheeks and loose around his jaw.

"Silly boy," she admonishes. "Everyone knows the Americans started it."

He shakes his head sadly. "No, a convenient fiction, one which serves the ongoing occupation. It was I who started that war, I and a woman who I suspect was a spy. She made love to me in a tent, to steal an officer's sword. The retribution he wreaked changed the direction of our mainland campaign, into our eventual confrontation with America."

At last! She mentally licks her finger and draws a mark – it's the cherry. She gives herself top marks for instinct.

"Why are you smiling?" He asks.

"She must have been quite a woman," she purrs, "to change the course of history."

He slams the table with his palm. "Don't patronize me!" He roars. The cups and bottles jump, and so does she, involuntarily from her knees onto her haunches. The whisky bottle rolls across the lacquered table top, emptying. She leaps to stop it, snatching the ever-ready towel from her sash. "I'm sorry! I'm sorry!" She yelps. Her hair comes loose as she wipes.

"You are the fool!" he continues. His face is red and twisted like a dog's. "I suppose you believe everything they tell you on this screen? Don't you know they use it to rot your mind?"

Then he picks up the webscreen's remote control and throws it at the wall, where it smashes into plastic shards. The screen falls black and silent. The remote spins across the floor, its innards sticking out. With heart beating, the thought again invades her mind – hand-held devices, Northern agents. Perhaps he isn't just endearingly crazy - perhaps he's dangerous. She sets the glasses right. What should she do?

"Have you seen the paintings of the courtesans of old?" He enquires furiously. "They lived behind paper screens in the Emperor's Palace, brushing their long hair in their silk kimonos, flashing an ankle here, a finger there, tempting suitors from the noble classes. This is you girl, with your cosmetics and practiced smiles and fabricated opinions. The court nobles fawned while their world was run by warlords and criminals, and nothing has changed in a thousand years!"

"You are right… you are right," she is reciting, head bowed, in a childish voice. "I am a fool." He has come here to cause trouble. He is an extremist or an anarchist. She will report him to Kovacs.

"You are living inside a screen covered in pretty pictures and words!" He continues loudly. "You've been lied to all your life!" He gestures to the walls, the garden, the bar. "Just ask the Emperor! I want to see the Emperor!" He thumps the table again.

"I am very sorry." Her eyes have narrowed. She was stupid to have imagined he was attracted to her, or that she should play along with him. He is a mad dangerous wolf. Now she will have to break her professional code of silence. She is trembling. She raises her head, and is surprised to see him now smiling at her benignly. Is this what happens when a sleepwalker awakes? She'd better let security assess him. She reaches under the table.

"Forgive me, Saori," he says with a kind of remorse. "I do not mean you personally, but everyone, the whole world…. it's the whisky, my memories…"

She smiles at him sweetly. "Don't worry, Ambrose dear. It is understandable. I spoke out of turn." Her finger presses the alarm button.

She quickly gathers the tray and the bottle and the broken remote, to make her escape. "Your hair is loose," he says with a frown. "My gift, like my manners, is poor."

"Permit me to redo it, and replace your order," she says, shuffling backwards.

She marches into the kitchen and pulls out her phone. She checks updates absently. The Giants are losing. The subways are closed. His temper, giving her the comb of an old dead woman – it was all too much. What is it about tonight? The guy at the bar smashing his phone. It's still on the counter where she left it. She hurls it, along with the Ambrose's remote, into the bin. She nearly follows them with the comb, but decides to keep it. She'll show it to Kovacs. It might be worth something.

The plastics group buzzes for more buckets of Cool Sweat. She combs her hair down and bumps into a guard on her way out.

"That problem customer? Last location?"

"Willow room," she reminds him.

"Negative. I've checked all rooms and the CATV. He's gone. Left his bill though," he gives her the cash and shrugs. She opens her phone and calls Kovacs.

*   *   *

I feel my way along the alley outside the Golden Lion Snack Bar, ready to dive amongst the trash – rotting kitchen bags, broken scooters, old pots, dumped appliances. Despite its outward gloss and wealth, Imperial City is full of decaying buildings and junk, as if no-one can bear to be rid of the past. Its alleys are full of last century's rusted plumbing and debris, plywood sheets and plastic litter. Blue tarpaulins paper over cracks in the walls and the building codes. Streaks of mildew stain the gutters and the crumbling earth walls, one of which I slip over and crouch behind. The security goons will soon be searching. *From Here On*
I Believe in Tomorrow

The Big Ears blimp has floated downtown amongst the corporate towers. Its screen is almost 3D in the steam rising from the vents. As I watch, the red and gold screen changes to a new motivational message:
Giants 2 Tigers 12
Better Luck Next Time!

With all our screens and playlists and cameras, we seem to be creating another layer of illusion. In the daily gloss of updates and plug-ins we are getting lost in a new image of ourselves – or making a new surface in which to gaze at our image. The sidewalk people are hooked to their phones; around the corporate logos and the soft-glow of the convenience stores, Imperial City's grid flicks on and off in a network. People groom themselves and go downstairs to the malls, where the plastic gardens and imitation chrome fittings mirror the luxuries shown on their plasma screens. Between the towers and airships, the screens keep multiplying and copying.

But with one click – a missile attack, a data-leak - it could all disappear. It has happened before and it will happen again. Imperial City is a phoenix, growing and decaying. Its true skyline is not in space but in time: flames are constantly licking out of windows while ghost-armies murder each other. It is one city buried beneath another, just like Saori in there is one person buried beneath another. Its history – and hers - is not joined up. There are many layers of pretty masks. Beneath this city is an entirely different one, screened away by the make-up and postures of the present.

A cat runs up to my fingers. It can smell the spoiled meals in the bins of the snack bar. As I made my unscheduled departure through the kitchen, I saw a bin left open, with the remote control that I broke lying in it, and a mobile phone too, so I pocketed them. Call it a Tanabata memento.

The cat mewls, arches its tail and runs down the alley, briefly looking back at me with eyes like candles. I pick up my cane and use it to slowly get up. I brush the sand from my tails and shuffle carefully over old bicycles and rusted wheel-rims. The night is humid. The pedestrian street, with its open cafes and manicured shop-fronts, looks like a beautiful silk ribbon tied around a decaying body. A dank mist hangs in the air. The jumbled warren of snack clubs is a low glow a hundred metres away. The thickening crowd of gorgers and shoppers gives me cover, so I walk as quickly as I can. Cameras will trace my steps, but a tantrum by a silly old man will soon be buried.

I check my watch and look up at the stars: Vega and Altair are approaching their zenith. It is time to move. Soon the Tanabata fairy will begin her song. Soon a bridge will open up through the illusions of screens and years, and we will see our true natures, unified. I have to get to Kirin Shrine, where the fairy dwells, to give thanks for my worldy fortune, which I found buried under a layer of rubble, on another Tanabata eve long ago. I pull up my trousers and adjust my hat. Big Ears updates:

Smile When You Are Going Your Way!

The Dig

An older version of the central City used to stand here, but it was incinerated in the last days of the Patriotic War. We are taught that the defeat and destruction of my country was a good thing: if allowed to succeed, our race would have committed unspeakable crimes; we would have plunged the world into endless conquest, enslaving our captives and imposing barbaric rule everywhere we went. But our victors grasped the flame and slowly burnt alive the terrible monster we had become.

As the smoke cleared and people were carried out, the absence of the buildings seemed to make room for peace to move in. Redemption seemed possible. People – even our enemies - saw our suffering, so compassion could appear again in the world. For a while, all that was impure was wrenched out of people's hearts.

Why does compassion require such terrible tragedy? Perhaps at our murky depths of consciousness, the truth appears as pairs of opposites which we can only grasp one at a time. Compassion and tragedy, love and hate, barbarity and justice, growth and decay are different measures of the same quantity. We experience a kind of optical illusion and we see the one separated into two. Perhaps one day we will focus our vision onto a clearer point where one thing doesn't split into two; where love cannot live alongside hate, prosperity doesn't mask injustice, and peace doesn't justify power: until then, we will always wonder how we got lost in the weird labyrinth of history.

Defeat was swift. Along with thousands of other troops I was brought back to the homeland from the battlefields, a prisoner. We found our families absent, our offices run by foreigners. Our leaders were dead or in exile. Our generals were dressed in dogs' masks and paraded through the streets. Our Emperor and his industrial families were made paupers. I was a prisoner of war on my own soil.

We were permitted to return to our neighborhoods. My home was a pile of debris in a landscape of rubble, my parents and sister nowhere to be found. A surviving neighbour recalled that my sister was sent north a year before, to a province that was not yet held by the Americans. Refugees from purges on the mainland were arriving in these Northern Provinces in illegal flotillas. They were fast becoming a hotbed of post-war instability. Among them were revolutionaries of every political stripe, ragtag armies, spies, smugglers and war criminals on the run. Bridges and communications were down; people were thrown back to tribal loyalty and international black markets; soon a guerrilla war with the occupiers began.

Stalemated by the steep terrain and civil infighting, the Americans cut their losses and withdrew to a demarcation they drew through the country. They focused their efforts on defending the new border towns, blockading the rebel ports, building up the walls around their Asian fortress: the democratic South.

They imposed martial law and an open market. They flew in plane loads of dollar bills and blue jeans. We got Big Ears the Mouse, Cool Sweat and a baseball league. They gave us free radios and general elections. They gave us wheelbarrows and shovels: you can see pictures of us standing there in our tattered uniforms, smiling in the acres of rubble, smoking. We were smiling not just for the camera, but because we were the survivors, the lucky ones, with a goal: to build a better world. Surrounded by horror, we dreamed. Such is the inconstancy of the human heart

We put on our occupier's clothes, we learnt his pop songs and adopted his icons. We saw the world through his eyes – and his eyes were the webscreens and 24-hour channels, the airship dishes and national curriculum; the doctored words of the constitution. We wore a foreigner's mask; the old society was buried and a new one created as effectively as a concrete pour over a mountainside. Our minds became like the streets we built and rode to work: engineered, drained and paved. We were individually free, but as a country we remained prisoners of war.

I was one of the thousands of workers in the Democratic Reconstruction Teams. We wore blue overalls and built perhaps the grandest residence ever created by humanity: the hi-tech megapolis of an industrialized nation. How rapidly this city sprouted from its torched remains; the vast towers, the hi-speed trains, the factories and grids, hospitals and highways, boutiques of cloth and cosmetics; dig by dig, pour by pour, one shovel load after another. Like history, the city is another slow accretion of individual acts, a self-organising cell that we are now only dimly aware we are part of. Back then, I helped start it, just as I'd helped end it.

In the Reconstruction Period I came across Mei Lee again. I was having breakfast one day in a construction team mess tent when her face leapt out from the newspaper. The beauty of her features carried through the graininess of cheap print - peasant girl, cripple, lover, foe - it was the woman I had made love to in Yamamoto's tent. But there was no palsied eye: she glared directly into the camera: the famous Madame X, the absent Committee Member, the Mother of the Revolution. One of the earliest rebel commandos, she'd disappeared in action a year after the September 18 Incident, her body never recovered. Her exploits as a saboteur and spy were a legend, and many believed her still alive. She'd been kidnapped by the Americans, she was in the Vietnamese politburo, she was masterminding the revolution from a secret mountain hideaway… I cut out the photo and its caption: "A chair will always be held empty on the Great Committee for our eternal comrade, the Bride of the People. May her wisdom and courage still lead the nation." I kept the photo in a pocket over my heart, which of course still bore the scar of my encounter with her.

Now that photo is reproduced on t-shirts and posters the world over, a talisman for rebellious teenagers, a figure of fun for jingoistic politicians – the same politicians who bog their countries down in endless wars. Madame X, an ironic icon for an apolitical age.

I salvaged a few possessions and pipes from my family house, hung tarpaulin between the walls, and began to rebuild. The house filled with refrigerators, TV screens, music players, gadgets of the better future. We laughed at our Northern compatriots' single-model cars, their rolling brown-outs, their backyard smelters. They lived in monolithic apartment blocks, had one TV station, and attended public parades every weekends. We had Hollywood, human rights, and endless freedom of choice. The North had communal dormitories, re-education farms, and the Great Committee. We had missile shields, fast food and corporate cartels. I kept digging, shovel in hand, crumpled photo close to my chest, the shining new walls around me shielding me from the x-ray of the truth.

*   *   *

We sometimes came across old foundations in the rubble, piles of antique pottery and sodden charcoal, old stepping stones, the remains of hand-hewn rock walls. Work ceased and the archaeological teams moved in. From these historical digs I learnt that underneath Imperial City's new roads and neighborhoods were other roads and neighborhoods, and beneath them, still others. As I said, this is one city buried beneath another, and with their shells, the Americans had cut a transect through the City's different eras. They had destroyed the present, yet exposed the city's ancient roots for all to see.

I found work with the archaeological teams on the pump and earth moving equipment, and often joined the students and professors crouching in the dust with tiny brushes and picks, sweeping clay dust from pottery shards, uncovering the city's foundations of lost homes and fallen shrines.

We found old warlords' villas. We explored cisterns for their waste and their garbage tips for rusted armour. I listened to the professors explain changes in artistic movements and philosophies from shards of pottery. From twists of copper they deduced the development of plumbing designs and trade routes. I began exploring the previous versions of Imperial City, finding the bones and belongings of the dead, walking down their streets, brushing their dust away from my clothes. I enrolled in history courses at the national university and helped the professors prepare artifacts for study.

I found a child at the bottom of a well, a man bricked up between two walls, a woman buried under a stone plinth. Murder victims perhaps; secret crimes of madness or political intrigue. From these, the central thesis of my future career began to form: most archaeological digs are crime scenes. The rows of skeletons in ancient mounds, the broken walls swallowed by forests - all reflect the great robberies and incursions of history. The remains of a city wall signify its sacking; a horde of treasure a royal line liquidated. Fallen columns and burial mounds are evidence of vice, neglect, criminal greed, over-reach.

The people whose skeletons we pieced together out of rubble expected these homes to be still standing, their descendents marking their tombs with cut flowers. They didn't expect their bones to be scattered, the life-dreams buried. Archaeology proves a life of peace or prosperity to be an unlikely fate. The sea of rooves we were constructing proves it: survivors will always put brick back on brick to create a fairytale of continuity.

July 7, Year 6 of the Emperor of Peaceful Harmony. Tanabata, Anno Domini 1959, twelve years after the end of the Patriotic War. I was working six metres below street level on a monastic hermitage destroyed during the Warring States Period. A pump was broken, threatening the foundations of a small teahouse on the edge of the grounds, and I was working late to save the structure from re-inundation. Everyone else had gone home to celebrate Tanabata with their families, or to public concerts to see aging courtesans singing the old songs, wearing tattered kimonos on makeshift stages. I had no family to return to, and no-one except me knew it was the anniversary of the Patriotic War, so I avoided all celebrations.

I worked by the light of a lamp, running the pump on and off, not really noticing the many sounds in the air: the festivals above me, the crackle of martial tunes bursting from loudspeakers in the nearby field dormitories, the twitter of birds flocking, the courtesans' voices, the parties where my colleagues drank wine and swapped pictures of girls… I didn't at first notice the melody wavering from quiet to loud - I was distracted by the pump's innards and it wasn't until I finally switched it off that I noticed how close the sweet song was. I immediately recalled the sunless rubble under the Marco Polo Bridge, the notes of a similar song, fireworks going off. I peered through the ruins half-expecting to see a woman wandering somewhere amongst the exposed walls.

I picked up my lamp and held it out – empty shadows leapt over banks of earth. The sheer walls pressed me in, and only the great arc of the milky way was visible above. The song was full of melancholy and heart-ache, yet there was a purity in the suffering, as if all care was gone. Perhaps the ghostly voice was a sonic illusion – concert sounds above magnified by the pit.

My chest began to itch around the scar left there years before. I tore open my shirt and found blood dripping from it in long lines. My shirt was stained; I remembered the newspaper picture of Mei Lee I kept there and trtied to save it. When I saw those sharp almond eyes, the pain in my heart knocked me to my knees.

In my faint I thought I saw American bombs landing, and my parents running from the flames. I saw the dogs feasting in Yamamoto's prison yard, and I saw the hermitage around me burning while monks closed the gates on people trapped within. I clamped my hands over my ears and the song remained.

"May all mortal flesh be silent…" the voice sang.

"A prayer for the cherubim." Another voice said.

I looked up but my lamp had gone out. I could see nothing in the pit.

"It's a hymn." The second voice said, even closer. I staggered to my feet, tense and ready to fight, my soldier's instincts still strong.

"Where are you?" I shouted.

A flint struck twice. The spark lit a small glow which was behind a red curtain. The red ball became a small carriage, illuminated from within, and soon lit the axles and harness of a rickshaw, in which a man stood, bare-chested, with a cloth around his waist. It was not this figure who was speaking, but another from the carriage.

"There are strict public safety ordinances in this city," it said. The curtain parted to reveal a large man sitting inside. He wore silks that were dusty and torn. He was pointing at the newspaper cutout that I'd dropped at my feet. He had a bulbous nose and grey bushy eyebrows, and I recognised the man I'd shared a cell with years before.

"No foreigners," he announced. "And certainly no littering."

"Marco Polo!" I was astonished.

"Oh, not again. It really is a matter of some urgency that you get off the street." He offered me his hand, which was sweaty from the humid summer night. The carriage swayed and rattled as he made room. He uncorked a gourd from which he took a quick sip before handing it to me. "Drink a little, not much." He took the newspaper picture from my hand.

"Did you say street?" I asked. "What street?"

He squinted at me, looked my overalls up and down, and sighed. "Go on, look out the window."

Outside was not the dark earthen walls of the dig, nor the modern structures of Imperial City, but a street full of wooden shop fronts, many shuttered at this hour, but some lit by small lamps. Small groups huddled on mats and cushions outside their shops, eating from small bowls or displaying wares on low tables. The tables contained a few beans, a few pieces of dried fruit, a few limp vegetables. Despite the late hour workers in thick clogs bore buckets of water through the mud. There were other curtained rickshaws like ours, dragged by strong-legged young boys and bow-legged old men. Behind the low wooden shops loomed the grand tiled rooves of hermitage buildings, their curved gables rising into the sky.

"It's the hermitage," I said. " It's the ancient city!"

"Indeed." He was smoothing out the picture of Mei Lee, "just as I suspected," he continued. "The saint." He turned the picture over, briefly examining in puzzlement the newsprint on the back.

"That's no saint!" I exclaimed. "That's Madame X, the Northern rebel leader, the missing member of the Great Committee."

He glanced at me, holding the picture lightly between two fingers. "Rebel, yes, missing, no. You must not be found with this image in this city, do you understand." He held the scrap over the lamp he had lit. "It is lucky you found me."

"I found you?"

He ignored me and the picture flared into yellow flame and floating black ash. "There," he said with some relief. He brushed down his clothes, then turned to me with a stern look. "Do not mention that woman again."

"But she's not…"

"Shhhh," he hissed, and opened a chink in the curtains. "Do you see those men?" Amongst the foot traffic stood men armed with curved swords, dressed in black cloaks, with finely-sewn crests.

"Secret police," said Marco Polo. "Hitmen is a better word. They are on the lookout for intruders, foreigners, spies such as yourself."

"But I'm none of those!"

"Look at how you are dressed!" I looked down at my dirty blue overalls, still hanging open, and I noticed that the scar around my heart had stopped bleeding. "That bizarre outfit alone would get you imprisoned and tortured without question. Especially tonight."

"How would I know what to wear?" I exclaimed.

"Weren't you the one who turned up in the Khan's territory dressed as an artilleryman?" He stifled a guffaw. "Oh yes, I was certain you would be executed. How did you get out of that one?"

"I just walked free," I explained. "Straight after you left I found my way back to my command and…er…" I fell silent as he giggled inappropriately.

"Found your way back? My friend, there is no way back. Wherever you ended up after we last parted was not the same place you left." He eyed me with amusement. "And what occurred when you found your command, hmmm?"

"A terrible war began…which, well, er… I started."

"You started a terrible war. And what else?"

"I lost my family."

"Uh huh." He kept nodding.

"My country was invaded and occupied."

"Pretty standard stuff," he claimed. "Go on."

"Now I'm helping build a better future, a new society."

"Of course you are. Of course you are," he smiled as if at a child. "Anyone close to you been raped, tortured or kidnapped?"

"A friend was beheaded, and my sister is missing, presumed to be in a mass grave."

"Yes, she probably is. Often feel alienated from your fellow citizens?"

I thought about it. "Yes. For example, no-one seems to understand tonight is the anniversary of the start of the war. "

"Exactly." he threw up his hands. "Are you able to make head or tail of history or your individual purpose within it?"

"Hmm, not really."

"Then you are still just as terribly lost as you were last time." He sighs in exasperation. "Completely adrift. I'm not surprised you've turned up again. The cycles continue. History is not a straight line, you see, but a bunch of layers, like a geological deposit. Events press on each other, push each other around. If an earthquake occurs," he slides one hand along the other, "past and present can re-align. Happens all the time. Discontinuities. Erasures of memory. Tall tales becoming historical fact." He tapped his head and winked; I was beginning to feel bemused by his enigmatic attitude. "I'm surprised you've chosen this particular time, to be honest. It's pretty horrid." He peeked carefully through the curtain again.

"I didn't choose anything."

He looked exasperated. "Can't you hear the singing?" Indeed the eerie song was still drifting from the street outside.

"It thought it was a concert," I commented.

He laughed. "It is, of a sort. It's a hymn, from the liturgy of St James."

"Who is singing it?"

He stared at me with a furrowed brow. Then sighed, "I suppose I will just have to show you." He rang a little bell on the rickshaw and it lurched into motion.

"And you, Mr. Polo?" I took the opportunity to change the subject. "How did you escape the Khan's custody?"

"Oh, there are various versions," he replied. "Which one would you like to hear?"

"The best one."

"Well said," he laughed, and cleared his throat. "Well, on learning of my good name, the Great Khan summoned me from his dungeons and commissioned me with a great task: to escort his fortieth daughter to her wedding, which he had arranged with a prince of a spice island far away in the southern seas. He provided me with four ships to carry the princess' train and collect tributes along the route. We set sail from Canton, and not even a comedian could conceive of the accidents we encountered.

"Firstly, the fleet captains, believing their journey to be an easy one, oversupplied the crew on the first leg, and we were forced to seek replenishment in the wild kingdoms of Fiju, a country usually avoided by navies and merchant men. The men of Fiju are bound by oaths and curses to fight with anyone not related to them; and in fact even distant relations – second cousins for example, or an uncle's uncle – required certain types of violent engagement. Foreigners of course are instantly slaughtered, however some pogrom or disaster must have affected the coastline we approached, for we found its port broken and its battlements undefended. So we stormed ashore and found the people there starving to death, and their wells poisoned. The only thing they had in great quantity was wine, which we stole and were forced to drink on the way to our first scheduled supply stop – the celebrated Archipelago of Mai.

"The now drunken fleet pitched up on the shore of the tribes of Mai who, unlike the brigands of Mibu, regard it as marvelous fortune to not just meet strangers, but to copulate with them. Their menfolk devote themselves to developing members of such unnatural length that they can swing them between their knees, while the women cultivate equally pendulous breasts, which they throw over their shoulders, and each other's shoulders too. They demand of each foreign lover only a bracelet of brass or copper, and those with the greatest number of bracelets are regarded as the most valuable in marriage. To the entire tribe's delight, two hundred drunk sailors now descended on their village, and the ensuing orgy may have been the end of our voyage, had we not accidentally poisoned their king, who drank such a long and continuous amount of the wine that he fell stone dead, and we were forced run back to our ships, unable to replenish our water barrels, or carry the boiled hippopotamus with which they had given us in tribute.

"Our next destination was the volcanic island of Anbon, where our fleet's reputation had preceded us, and we were repelled by cannon, though a night raid looted a few coconuts and yet more liquor barrels. So we diverted to Cebu, and at this midpoint of our journey, amid the boiling equatorial seas, our captains and their mates all fell dead of a fever. Their affliction, some said curse, sped through all four ships, unhappily mitigating the food supply problem as its victims died in the most alarming way – falling from their posts foaming at the mouth, their limbs turning black – and the rest were saved only by multiple amputations.

"We were now off course, un-captained, half-manned and constantly drunk, and when we reached Cebu, an unrelenting storm descended, shattering our masts and sinking two ships with all hands. For several weeks the broken fleet frantically sought anchorages amongst the rocky islets and wild currents, and every time we managed to seek supplies ashore, the landing parties were set upon by gangs of giants. These were wild men, ten feet tall, covered in manes of red hair, wielding jagged harpoons with which they gutted our landing crews, and fed their bleeding limbs to the giant lizards which they kept as pets. With ferocious gangs patrolling the shores, and whirlpools controlling the sea, we were forced to cling to shallow reaches and reefs, eating penguins while the men aboard weakened from scurvy.

"By the time the weather lifted, our numbers had been reduced again by half. Nontheless we continued, straight into a fleet of Javanese pirates, who mercilessly boarded and raped us all, then took us to their secret cove, where they betrothed the Khan's daughter and her train to the pirate king. Their great undoing was a bizarre ceremony in which the bridegroom had to ride a horse with silver shoes onto a precipitous cliff in the mountains, and stand on its back for the reading of the vows. Before the final vow the prince's horse slipped on its shoes and both man and beast plunged headlong onto the rocks five hundred feet below. In the ensuing chaos we fought our way back to our ships. The pirate fleet pursued us, and captured one of our ships, which seemed to satisfy them, as they gave our ship up, probably thinking us cursed. I found myself in charge of a crew of fifteen sick men and the Princess, with no choice but to continue to her true wedding.

"I studied my precious maps. I planned to ride the trade winds to the Moluccas but with such a small crew I was at the mercy of the currents, and the elements dragged me north, east and west, but rarely south. With no knowledge of longitude, we were soon hopelessly lost. On the fourth month we spied a row of volcanic isles, where dusky women danced on the beaches. Our spyglasses revealed palm-frond hamlets, and baskets deep with tropical fruit. The entire crew leapt overboard, but only two made it to the beach, where they were hoisted onto the shoulders of the men and carried into circles of naked women and wild drummers, never to be heard of again.

"I was left alone with the Princess. We sailed on helplessly, unable to walk on the pitching decks from weakness and exposure, eating leather and sackcloth from the rigging to stop our bodies starving. Weeks later we hit a wild storm of such intensity I was certain it would finish us off, and indeed prayed that it would. I tied myself and the Princess to the remaining mast and passed into hopeful delirium.

"The typhoon didn't sink the craft, but nudged it fortuitously into the lee of an island. Thieves from the nearby port spied the listing vessel and sailed out to loot it, but were alarmed when the two corpses aboard came back to life. We were delivered to the local warlord, who assumed we were Spaniards. Spain was by then sending boatloads of saints to the island, to save its souls and prepare it for full-scale invasion. They had told the Emperor that they were the spiritual masters of a peaceful and united globe, and had been authorised by God to deliver Him and his subjects to Heaven. In a few short translated words I relieved him of this fairy tale, and informed him of the true ambitions of Christendom. The Emperor set about bloodily expelling the foreigners, while I was granted a large country estate and permission to marry the Khan's daughter. So here we are, both living in glory as saviours of this nation, the exact location of which is kept secret, as its Emperor quite sensibly wishes no further commerce with the outside world."

*   *   *

Marco Polo sat for a while staring at the bustle outside, as if lost in contemplation, but then fluffed up his silk kimonos and sternly pronounced: "So that was how, starved, shipwrecked and expecting death, we changed history without even trying. In fact it was the very novelty of the events we set in train that gave them such power to influence. This is how the tiny, unique lives of individuals are magnified by the divine, invisible winds that blow us between life and death, giving us the power to create the world itself."

"Is that your theme?" I countered a little too argumentatively, as I had been sipping from the gourd throughout. "Isn't it a little far-fetched? Aren't the facts just a little exaggerated for me to draw that conclusion?"

He glared at me, visibly upset. "Well, allegory as a form is always a risk, but my method is to describe a series of events, giving them the status of fact or history, and then to draw universal conclusions, in order to illuminate the murky relations between universal truth and temporal fact."

"Narrative theories." I scoffed. "Surely just reporting the basic facts is extreme enough? Exaggeration pushes them into the realm of make believe."

"Exactly!" He cried, snatching back the gourd and wetting his throat. "Where narrative best belongs. Fantasise! Mythicate! Stretch the imagination! This is the art of the storyteller: to make me believe the impossible! Then, when my eyes are dazzled and my mind soft and pliable under the spell of its own imaginings, you can transform it with your moral, shock my soul into a new paradigm. Young fellow, in my experience, human beings do not learn easily. We remain in the rut of our own and others' thinking, like this rickshaw: it runs in the smoothest path possible – that made by the habit of others. Even if it is headed to a dead-end or disaster, we will only avoid it by accident or mistake. People have to be blind-sided with the truth to learn - otherwise they do not accept it as true. People are rarely convinced by explanation or argument – these things merely deepen the rut, by forcing counter-argument and defensive thinking. Realism – bah! - pandering to people's delusions, a blind repetition of what is already believed. Let unrealism be your method – mystify, lullify and hypnotise your audience with dreams and confusions, then run them through with the short sharp sword of truth."

As I pondered this I realised the hymn outside had grown louder, and had been joined by many other voices. There was the sound of a large crowd.

"There's not much time," my interlocuter said. "I have one more story for you."

"Now?" I asked.

"No. You will find it back in the teahouse, where you bumped into me tonight."

"The teahouse?" I was astonished. "What kind of story is it?"

"I don't know yet," he shrugged. "I haven't written it."

At this point the vehicle stopped, and the rickshaw driver called out that we had reached a bridge over the river. The hubbub of voices around us had increased.

"You're not a Christian are you?" He enquired.

"I most certainly am not."

"Good. We have a little spectacle to attend." He opened the curtains: we were at a grand bridge - the bridge that leads to Kirin Shrine, where my family held a picnic earlier tonight - and a crowd was gathering on both banks of the river. There was a celebratory feel in the air, and everyone was listening to a choir performing on a little stage on one bank, which was illuminated by a circle of lanterns. I could tell from the great number of swords and crests that many gathered near the stage were nobility. Each chorus member had bared feet and a bald head, and wore a simple blue gown. As I listened, enjoying the pure voices, I noticed that the central member was beautiful, as beautiful as…

"The saint," my friend whispered. "Singing Christian works in defiance of the Emperor's command." From that distance, by the light of the lanterns and through the dense evening crowd, the central figure looked like Mei Lee in yet another disguise, not a peasant brigand nor the revolutionary Madame X, but a cenobite, her face lit by the experience of god, or of longing to be with her saviour.

"*May all mortal flesh be silent…*" she sang.

"Saint who?" I asked.

"She goes by no other name." He shrugged.

"*…and with fear and trembling stand…*"

More choral singers had moved onto the stage, but they were not gathering voluntarily. About thirty more frocked and shaved singers were climbing up chained together at the waist and ankles, and some of the audience around the stage were not dressed in fine gowns and crests, but in hoods and leather masks. As my eyes fully adjusted to the scene I realised what was happening. The stage was built on top of thick layers of faggots. It was a pyre. They were going to be burned.

The chattering of the crowd grew more agitated as some men in black kimonos – secret police - rode horses across the stream and dismounted. They began shouting at the penitents, jeering and angry, to cheers from the audience. Then one officer unrolled a scroll and began reading. My companion closed the curtain a little more. "If you do not want to watch," my companion whispered in my ear, "I understand."

They began painting the prisoners with black pitch to ensure they burnt well. The tar was smeared over their faces, arms and legs. The chains were pulled tight, and tied to the back of the stage. The voices of some prisoners faltered as they were pressed into an amorphous mass, but the saint's impassioned soprano leapt forth, firing their wills.

"That the powers of hell may vanish, as the darkness clears away."

Some of the prisoners fainted, dragging others down. The officer stopped reading and an expectant silence fell across the crowd, except for single voices praying in Latin, invocations to Deus, Maria, Christos. A leather man crawled under the stage with a brazier and smoke began to rise.

"A man who has breathed bad air falls into a fever to expel the infection," Marco Polo commented. "This country has fallen into a fever, and is trying to right itself. Of course it is not right that these people suffer like this, but it is their own decision; they are in fact proud to die for their beliefs."

"How can you say so!" I gasped. "They are being murdered!"

He gripped my arm. "No, they think they have found a way out of this world. They believe themselves saints, blessed, the purest beings in the world. Meanwhile," he laughed, "their murderers believe themselves great benefactors and lawmakers. They are, executed and executioner, locked together as a unit, a testament to the enormous power of delusion, the true God of this world."

As the screaming started, the saint's voice miraculously rose higher, more powerful than before.

"The awful spectacle here is our nature revealed. As you look upon it, try to understand that all is right with the world. Suffering begats suffering, false belief creates false belief, truth breeds truth. It's a wonderful, barbarous, savage realm. Look, off they go, destroying themselves in the only way they know how." He smiled benignly. "Who is next? You? Me? We are all for the abyss. What a wonderful world."

Flames were climbing up bones. Bodies were popping and screaming. Limbs and torsos were jerking out of the column of smoke and falling back in. I shuddered and watched as the people cheered, and the flags waved and black smoke climbed into the air. The horrified, happy, gloating faces reflected a world trapped inside itself. All were contorted in pleasure or writhing in pain, decaying, burning, crumbling into dust. All were attending this feast alone, ignorant of the ultimate truth of their existence, soon to fall back into the bottomless pit of fire. The smoke blew across my face, stinking of meat. My vision started to crumble. Obscured by twists of smoke, the city and its horde faded and disappeared.

*   *   *

I woke in the rubble with the sun rising in my eyes. I was next to the teahouse, where I had been working the previous evening. The pump drummed in the air, operating at full capacity. Had I fixed it, after all? Had I slept exhausted, dreaming of my fantastic companion and the pyre - phantoms of my trauma from the war? The muddy sump where the teahouse foundations lay was now empty and a collection of rubbish was exposed: sodden beams and splinters of timber, rusted metals, bowls, scraps of leather. One piece caught my eye: a copper cylinder half buried in the mud. Remembering Marco Polo's words of the previous night - *"I don't know yet. I haven't written it"* - I leapt into the pit.

The copper was dissolving into blue-green rust, but the cylinder was etched with pictures of animals – tiger, horse, rat – all the familiar animals of the years. Breaking the rules, I twisted the lid. Inside were parchments, covered in hand-written characters. I tipped one out, and before it crumbled in my hand, I saw the script was from the Warring States period, five hundred years before.

I put them back and placed the lid back on, and showed the cylinder to the Professors when they arrived. They were very excited, and took it to their department, and found inside a diary written in the hermetic script of the period. Owing to my interest they took me on to help with the painstaking task of piecing together the fragments. I studied the old characters as I worked, and earned my first degree with a translation of the scroll.

The Teahouse Scroll

Nothing disturbs the twilight but the dance of the stream, the ghosts of trees. The moon rises - a princess robed in carnation mist. Deeper, higher, the layers peel away. There is a tuneful modulation in the air like voices singing. It could be coming from three mountains away. It could be the blood in my veins. My thoughts and feelings scratch inside me, at once an irritation and titillation on the inner surface of my body. My memories of the city and the temples, my feelings for my brothers there; my knowledge of this or that – they are a throb of tissue, a faint glow. These sensations define the points where I separate myself from the world. I draw the boundary of myself, a mental line but there is really no division – it is merely a limit of awareness. I expand this sensory bubble into a festival of colour, a puppet show that I have acted out all my life. But now the strings have been cut.

*

Every branch is drawn in snow. Every twig is a finger in the grip of ice. I step into the silent white forest and gather wood. Snow breaks from the cedars, leaving rainbows glittering. The endless branches of body and mind. I look through the drifting thoughts that remain - I could say they are mine, but they are not.

*

Footfalls in the snow. Every day I wash my puppet garments, the costumes of my personal drama. I gather them around me like a robe tied tight to create the image of a person. I break ice in the washing bucket, see the body floating there. The costumes and lines of my personal drama bring me into being. I slap linen onto stone, not trying to rid myself of dirt, nor parade in front of others as a worthy man - more like a harlot in a downtown bar, stripping away my status, my name, my garments, to reveal the basic fact of nature. Me-less, faceless, universal.

*

Twigs break into my brazier. My hands look like snaky roots digging the earth. Hunger and cold are equidistant sensations, as ever-present as snowy peaks. Outside, the mountain ridges fold themselves into mist. Single trees poke through, like charcoal brushstrokes, each one representing the all. There is a smudge of gold in the sky: the sun, like a piece of statue in the corner of a temple.

*

I was looking for tubers and fungi when my fingers began to freeze. I swayed and clapped in the forest trying to get the thin webs of blood in my hands moving again. Down on the plain the sun was setting below a bank of clouds, casting a bronze glow across the fields and rivers. I could see a chain of low hills there, like the tail of the mountain swinging into the distance. As I flexed my wrists, sinuous movements spread up my arms, removing the tension from my muscles. As my nerves stretched, the mountain rose like a warm sap into my body. A triangle of light formed in my mind, reflecting the bronze mirror of the sunlit plain. I saw and felt: the triangle was my body - and the mountain energy rose up it like a snake toward the bright orb of the sun at its apex. For a moment the bronze plain, my twisting body; the mountain dragon, the river, the warm sun, the peak – all were one.

*

The temple was black and their chanting bodies disappeared, leaving just the song. The voices pushed the streams of incense into shapes - misty whorls dancing in Vedic letters. For eight hours our trance was a bridge out of this world. In the morning the head priest stood outside in his long robes. We bowed in the dust. My wife stood behind him, a boy wriggling in her arms, the only one of us smiling, trying to grab her nose. She stared at the cobblestones. I couldn't touch anyone, so I knelt, hands clasped: "It is finished. The pretence of me." She shook her head and a tear flew. All I saw in her face was the blood and sweat of the world; the meat wheel turning. It turned in her arms too: my son, my attachment to that wheel, to its circles of sorrow and joy, love and hate, it was bondage, pure torture. No longer could I build my life out of those opposites.

"We will free each other in the end," I said to them. Then I walked between crumbling walls into a bullock cart, and have not met the eye of a single human since.

*

The bullock cart lurched through the streets. I sat within, curtained; I heard the market cries - the merchants' lies, the croaking of beggars, the whores' promises, the squawk and squeal of animals. I had once thought this city so civilised – the clothes and coiffures, the industry and craft, the salons and mansions, the schools of art and state. Now it seems just detritus heaped up by those who are lost in distraction.

I closed the curtains. The goods and wares outside the window were grease for the meat wheel, but I felt myself released to a more glorious fate. The cartwheels beneath were spinning on a different axis, along the true road - the one to liberation. How I longed to ascend the leafy glades and silver streams to my four mat hut, its blackened kettle, a window overlooking ridges of pine. I had before me the glorious vistas of solitude, all the horizons of the world to visit.

*

I have nothing to drink but a cloud, nothing to eat but the fruits of the forest. I am freer than all the lords of the world. I run over the mountains in straw sandals, harvesting mushrooms, sleeping on moss, drinking the rivers. With my eyes on the backs of my eyelids, I am as natural as the trees or the stars. The crimson beams of the hut run with honey and wine. The clay cup in my hand holds oceans of colour. My daily handful of rice is a like a royal banquet. My preparation is complete.

*

I have seen others up here wandering the paths like deer, often naked, with unkempt hair. I have found one who has achieved the goal. In a forest glade darkened with the leaves of figs and creepers he was seated on a rotting platform. Surrounding his throne was an array of bamboo taps buried in the pine trees, trailing drips of red and yellow resin. His body was hard as varnished wood, his hide golden, his fingernails curved in milky scimitars. I could not tell whether the flesh was dead, because I thought I could hear a subtle breath – the sound of mind faintly touching matter. The resin had frozen his body, and his spirit was about to escape its coffin. I sat in awe of this achievement: this being was no longer human at all.

Staring at the lacquered skin, looking for signs of mutability – a falling hair, the flicker of a finger – I suddenly heard again the distant voices. Were they emerging from the stiff body, like an echo from one world to another? Were they reaching us here by some trick of the air or of memory? The resonant voices vibrated deep in my bones. Were they the brothers' beautiful chant, from so long ago? Why have they stayed constant, like a standing wave in my heart? It is a deep and dangerous attachment, which I should have rid myself of long ago. How I have failed!

*

I began to eat from the taps of resin. It was soft and chewy and hard to swallow. It tasted of sour wine, of the age of trees and the musty lairs of animals. I broke away chunks of amber sap. They changed my dreams and eyes. I stared for hours at a tree, or a pile of moss, and saw the energy shimmering within, obliterating the separate parts into a continuous, sinuous wave.

*

I am a layer of tissues, constantly experiencing separation. The tissues tickle and suck, pulse and throb, parts of the cosmos constantly birthing other parts. The body experiences separation whereas the cosmos it is a part of doesn't. Light and energy pass from the unified cosmos to the material tissue of the senses and this journey is a descent into darkness. The world is spirit entombed in matter; the one divided into many. But go beyond the bodily senses and I can strip layers of illusion away. The more layers removed, the more connected I am to the cosmos.

*

When I was a novice my job was to strike the temple bell to mark certain hours and duties. The hollow sound would spread over the temple grounds like a wave, lifting the mind of anybody who heard it, bringing them into its perfect circle. We were taught that the bell was a purifying force, bringing us back into the moment, reminding us of the power of present action over pre-conception.

Like all facts this teaching disappears under scrutiny to reveal a deeper layer of meaning. As I sit here in isolation I see my body as a bell reverberating and ringing with all the events of the past – events good and bad that I am holding onto to make the image – the sound – the vibration – of me. All these images and events in the mind have a prior cause, and in turn a present reaction, like the restriking of the bell. The bell demonstrates the process of illusion: the renewal of the false self in every present moment.

The mind in its un-struck state is quiet and free of reaction. It is free of the world-creating, self-deluding cycle. It has direct access its nature. It is the un-struck mind which is pure.

*

We were taught that because our thoughts were with the dharma, we could not strike an unjust blow. We were taught that our lord was a liberator, a man of peace who would rebuild the temples, renew the streets and canals, and establish just laws. Under his hand, the city would be cleansed. We were taught that the karmic sum of the City's past transgressions was war and conflict, and now these stains must be removed.

The worldly states were at war. We marched down from the temples under banners raised to mercy and compassion. We streamed from the rocky tracks with tongues of fire – pitch, cannon, gunpowder, knives – chanting the sutras of liberation. We were an army of monks unleashed upon the material world. As novices we had sat and absorbed the blows of wisdom, and now we would deliver those same blows on the townsfolk, and shatter their illusions. What a triumph of the false self!

*

Throughout the years of war the townsfolk had built ramparts around their neighborhoods to keep marauding armies out. The city was a maze of muddy dykes and rotting slums. The rusty barricades were defended by lame men and children.

Our cleansing process was simple. Fiery arrows breached the ramparts. The first out were rats, followed by beggars. These were cut down. Then we ran into the smoke-filled alleys and the real work began. Children were separated into classes. Women and animals were lamed and bound. Men and goods were labeled and counted. The city was divided it into this and that commodity, so much meat, so much gold. The old were taken to the fields. The sick were thrown in holes. We were cooks and chefs peeling and cutting ingredients, boiling them down and mixing, producing a whole from a disorder of parts. Superfluous persons were hoisted, opened and ground down. Warehouses were filled and set alight. Skewered bodies piled in empty lots. A deep fog descended and our activities became indescribable, unrecorded except in the annals of spirit.

The city simmered into one body, in agony at one place, in orgasm at another, emptying of vomit, filling with blood. Victim and victor were cured together in an obliterating frenzy. When our knuckles clenched, flesh fell from bone. We who thought ourselves beyond the meat wheel pulled bodies from its rim, locked legs in its spokes. We ruined ourselves with triumph.

The smoke blew away and opened the ruins to a clear sky. We walked through the rubble, broken. The mission was to destroy the city's past and create a pure civilization, but our hearts were what we utterly defeated.

How difficult and mysterious a road is Truth? How useless men's knowledge of it, that even the best trained can steer themselves back into hell?

*

Up on this mountain I have been repeating the mistake of the war. I have been trying to destroy my false self like the warrior I once was, to lift a sword of pure consciousness and cut it away, to leave a smoky ashy field on which to rebuild a greater me.

The warlord self-love has been in control all along, marching me up here and putting the sword of self-improvement in my hand, when there is no self to deny or improve; no ego to destroy.

*

By renouncing the world I have declared my separation from it, which is the true illusion. I cannot improve my nature by escaping worldly problems, but by holding onto them and feeling them struggle. I have been blocking my ears with resin, blinding myself with meditation, but the voices in my bones, the sensations in my heart were the inescapable 'me' all along: if the world is corrupt then so am I; if I am suffering, then so is it. The me I tried to destroy by marching up this mountain is the world I tried to destroy by marching down it. Both my attempts at escape and annihilation have bound me further to what I cannot annihilate.

*

Now I listen, and the voices and sensations of the past are still buzzing within, imperfect, impure, but in harmony, because I am no longer trying to escape. The harmony also contains the screams of the boys I stabbed, the women I raped, and all we continually create and destroy in our fog of ignorance and fear. For these things are now part of the whole. There is no escape.

*

I have finally become lost in the endless parts and wholes around me. Water flows through me from cloud to river. I and the trees are temporary houses for the same air. The origins of every creature is within another. We are not born into the world, but grow out of it. We share the same material and nature.

*

I long for the path back to the city. I think of my wife raising our son there, shedding blood, sweat and tears, sharing with me the harvest of our actions. In time, our hands will age into claws; the food we eat will blacken our bodies into sickness and disease and the water we bear from the communal well will be at times sweet and at times bitter. After we die the temple bell will continue to cast its fog across the slums, while the householders toil and the monks renew their broken vows. All will walk on the one true road that passes through every living body, that connects city to mountain, right to wrong, heaven to hell. There is no other road.

*

I awoke this morning looking from a rock ledge into a pool of water. There, amongst the reflected peaks, I saw a clear image of myself. The mountains shuddered and a ripple passed through my image, and I was gone. Only water remained. The water flowed downstream. It poured down the rocks into the valley, past the fields and temples and factories, under the bridges unnoticed, inseparable from the stream, undefined. I am gone. I never was. There's no possibility I could ever be.

*   *   *

Was it fact or fiction? Had Marco Polo really placed the scroll there in the teahouse foundations for me to find centuries later? If so, did he write it, or just pick it up on his travels? Either way, is it a work of experience or imagination?

Whatever the truth, it remains now in a glass case, part of the national canon, dehumidified, celebrated yet rarely read. So its letters fragment once again.

There's another question I ponder. *There is no way back* - Marco Polo had referred to my first Tanabata time-shift - *wherever you ended up after we last parted was not the same place you left.* Is this the same world I left when Marco Polo's rickshaw appeared mysteriously out of the shadows? After I climbed out of the excavation pit the next morning, the scroll decaying in my hands, all appeared unchanged. American airships floated through the dawn pink clouds, Imperial City's new glass towers and concrete motorways gleamed in the postwar sun. Reconstruction workers were asleep in their portable dorms, and their penniless children roamed the alleyways. If it was a different world, it was a seamless copy of the original. When I returned to my half-built shack there were the same miserable belongings inside: scavenged pots and bowls; a wobbly table, a picture of my sister on the makeshift mantel, and my one memento from the war – the chrysanthemum pattern, turtle-shell comb I recovered from the floor of Yamamoto's tent, after Mei Lee's robbery. The only thing missing, naturally, was the picture of Madame X from the top pocket of my overalls, burnt the previous evening, along with its subject.

I never got another one, as the Wall soon went up between the North and South, and a news blackout fell. We received only rumours from over the border, unconnected and hard to verify: the Great Committee had risen to power through a series of purges. The Members had near-godlike status; giant posters of them hung on the buildings which the citizens had to salute. They had covert eugenics factories breeding child soldiers to man the border. This is what we were told. The Americans began to root out insurgents and 'sleeper agents' from the North, and interview any citizen with family or business connections there. Our compatriots had become our nemeses. Because I had made enquiries about my sister, I was investigated and given a clean bill of civic health. They told me she could be in a re-education camp, or a factory. or … the Committee branded some refugees from the occupied South 'broken vessels', spoiled by their bourgeois life before the war, and executed them.

But now… did I really have a sister at all? Perhaps she'd been left behind in the world that existed before I met Marco Polo, and accidentally started the War. And what of Mei Lee? Was she really the legendary Madame X? Or had the world I met her in also been lost to the changing years? I often dreamed of her perfect beauty, her smooth body, her lover's cries. I imagined we'd conceived a child on the floor of Yamamoto's quarters, one that was now rising through the ranks of the Great Committee. Was my child one of the figures who plotted our destruction? I looked at the faces of these reviled men and women for traces of my family line.

Whether new world or old, the Reconstruction Teams kept shifting rubble mountains and raising steel bridges. Hydroelectric dams and international airports rose in our wake. The fog of war slowly cleared, and I swapped my blue overalls for professorial tweeds. At the re-opening of the National Museum, the Teahouse Scroll was selected to be in the inaugural exhibition, as an example of cultural treasures uncovered by the razing of Imperial City. During the opening ceremony the Emperor rewarded the University a sum that expanded the Department and secured my tenure.

When I rebuilt my house I put Mei-Lee's fallen kanzashi-comb and the photo of my sister on my new polished mantelpiece in my modernised kitchen, alongside a map of my country without borders and partitions, the way it used to be. The three objects make a kind of household shrine - a Tanabata shrine, a shrine to time and its shifting years - and every Tanabata since I have wandered up here to thank the Emperor for my fortune, and Marco Polo for his tales, and to pray for the safe return of those three things I miss the most.

The Satellite Launch

I step through the red arched gate and walk along a
path lined with stone lanterns. The city lights
twinkle through the trees. Around me is the jungly
buzz of cicadas in the shrine's forest. I fish a small
coin out of my pocket and toss it into the shrine's
collection box. Throughout Imperial City there are
shrines: swept cedar groves between the forest and
the town, sealed off by white ribbons and red arches.
They are a temporary exit from temporal life; these
shrines divide the human world from the wilderness.
Here you are not your name or your role, but a
creature on your hind legs, somewhere between birth
and death.

Eons ago, beyond memory, we gave up the forest
for field, the canopy of trees for a row of rooves, and
the rule of nature for the rule of Emperors. Over
millennia we descended into the streets and theatres
of the world, and with every structure left behind a
bit of our nature – a part of ourselves we needed to
forget - our fox nature, our snake nature, so we left it
here, encased in the dark box in the centre of the
Shrine, surrounded by flowers and fruit and incense.
This bit of soul, universal soul, is the god of the
grove, and when I toss my coin and clap my hands
to awaken it, I feel it is of course me that should also
be waking up.

I study the fine wooden panels of the reconstructed
shrine buildings, which are modeled on the long-

houses of tribal villages. They are not the original ones of course: after the War the entire complex was rebuilt from the City's original plans, which are kept inside the Imperial Palace. You have to understand that the entire city is a simulacrum, a copy of the original template, all its components replaced bit by bit over the centuries. You could say the same for its people - isn't this the lesson of the god of the grove? As descendents of the forest, aren't we endlessly evolving copies of what came before? Facsimiles of an original ancestor? Our senses, our thoughts, our creations all have as their master source something eternal, and in replicating it, make that source eternal.

So what did those first humans put inside the Shrine's casement box? A graven image? Dragon bones? An empty void? No-one dares look.

They say in the first shrine inside the Palace, the central casement contains a mirror that was left behind by the Sun Goddess, when she created the Earth and gave birth to the races of men. Since that last brilliant glance, no-one has ever gazed in this mirror. It has been kept in a layer of cloth, and every twelve years wrapped in another layer of cloth by the priests, for thousands of years. What better metaphor is there for the compounding of human ignorance? Deeper and deeper our link to the universe gets buried in layers of time and action. We are the Sun's imprint on Earth in material form - but now there is darkness. Mysteries lie in these Shrines, true mysteries because no-one can see them.

Kirin Shrine is built on the hill from where the first Imperial City was surveyed, one thousand five hundred years ago. The ancient geomancers believed the mountains were fiery dragons, which at certain places plunged their necks out of the ground, occupying the spirit of a waterfall or a rock. Kirin Shrine is built amongst exposed cliffs of buckled sedimentary rock, and the mazy red fences that necklace the shrines seem to reflect fire. It's hard to believe now, looking at these planted trees and model buildings, that ancient geomancers stood here and released dragons into the streets of the future capital. Streets were gridded, waterlines preserved, land contoured to bring the tellurian flow to the feet of the Emperor and his people. Now observe their creation: an orb of electricity flowing in abundance, vehicles moving through the nightscape like pearl strings through a jewel box, a floating world of wind and water.

Giant magnets spin underground, powered by atoms. Screens and information emerge from the flow. The atoms disappear into the void. The information constantly updates. Treasured by huge corporations, protected by industrial armies, legislated by governments, all this geomancy and history, economy and alchemy creates an entity we are barely aware of: a world built on a void; a floating world that's about to pop.

There is a rumble in the Northern sky. Behind the mountain range glows the distant orb of the Occupied Zones. Perhaps it's another drone raid? Then I see the flicker of a tail, and a red ball rises above the shadow of the range. A dragon? A Tanabata firework? Stratospheric exhaust hangs below it in the air. Another ball rises, then another. The three distant flames expand and head south. These are not dragons or fireworks: these are Northern rockets, aimed at us.

The response from Imperial City is immediate. I see airships across the city rising rapidly to defensive positions. Through waves of urban noise, the city's loudspeakers open with a squawk and discordant alarm tones begin to peal across nearby neighborhoods. Orange lights wink on and off across the city – traffic signals switched to cautionary mode. The air splits as two burning red engines roar overhead. They bank steeply and climb like hornets over the northern mountains. Other jets begin circling the city like fireflies.

The three balls still cross the sky with relentless purpose, growing brighter as they approach. Cars are slowing to a stop - a newscast is underway. From my shrine vantage point I can see small crowds gathering outside open shops and restaurants. Drivers are hunched over their cabin TVs. The networks will immediately declare that the launches are a political decoy by the Northern regime to blackmail its neighbours. The North will announce they are communications satellites, constructed by and for The People, to broadcast homeland culture and patriotic songs to the Occupied Southern Province. Commentators will state the North doesn't have the industrial base to produce such technology. Their education systems are not up to scratch. They are hobbled by ideological aims and academic defections. No broadcast has ever been picked up; there is footage of rocket debris being plucked from the sea.

Whatever the truth, these launches serve the purposes of both regimes. The North makes an impact on the international stage; the South boosts its defence industries budget. Both win the propaganda war they wage on their citizens.

Sound trucks have begun to patrol the neighborhoods, blaring warnings that amount to threats. "An attack on the city is underway. Stay indoors. Authorised personnel will soon secure your neighborhood." This is the beginning of a curfew. Safety Teams will soon be on the streets in their boots and helmets, cheerfully shouting slogans and questioning anyone out of doors. I should immediately take a cab home. An airship approaches the hill: Big Ears listening for footfalls and scanning for unauthorized behaviour. I don't want them to know I am here, wandering about at night, a suspicious infra-red glow on the hillside. I step into the forest and gaze up: the rockets are now flying between the Tanabata stars, three silent dots following each other. Diplomats and Secretaries of State across the globe will be conferring and drafting responses; secret codes will be entering defense systems; military fingers will be hovering over buttons. I sigh: its going to be a long night. The airship rattles past the hill. Its screen displays:

Opinions are United:

Freedom Is Our Dream

*   *   *

There was a single carriage trip to her grandparents' village: cold, mountainous country, serviced by narrow roads and a small railhead. There was a musty leaning wooden house, an ancient couple in aging kimonos patterned with fading flowers. There were creepers covering the trees, the screech of cicadas. The bay was slimy with seaweed. There was a row of trawlers behind the concrete breakwater, as ugly as the cheap restaurants lining the promenade, where the villagers dried fish and long white radishes to dry.

She was bored and homesick There were no other children in the streets, just old people. The village had an air of decay and collapse. She climbed with her grandfather and mother up a staircase into the mountain. The path was flanked with the trunks of ancient cedars and overhung with lush bamboo swaying in the breeze. They occasionally stopped to rest on small wooden platforms placed next to stone plinths carved with characters – quotations from gods and legends. She had the feeling that they were walking into the world of the ancients, and when they passed through a row of bright red arches, the crimson light surrounded them, and the whispering silence of the forest with the sun twinkling down through the leaves – it seemed they'd left behind the grimy outer world of the lonely village, and entered a purer realm – a realm where she belonged.

But the shrine buildings, like the village below, were falling into disrepair. Weeds grew on the moss-covered rooves. Wooden posts were pocked by insect borers. Scattered around the grounds were long-dead offerings of rotted flowers, stained cups spilling rainwater. The collection barrier, where people once threw small coins as an offering, contained only mud and discarded cigarettes. Her mother removed them and rang the bell to alert the spirits a wish was being made – it clunked in a sad, clogged up way - and her mother cried out and let go of the rope. A stream of insects dropped out of the bell and onto the ground around them. Disgusted, they cried out and backed away. More cockroaches streamed off the roof. Soon the shrine was covered by black shapes scurrying up the walls and across the beams, long feelers waving, disturbed by this unexpected visit from below.

One fell into her hair. She screamed and spun. It wriggled on her neck. She flicked it away. Her mother wrapped her hand in a handkerchief, wet it with her spittle, and began wiping her face…. Then suddenly the tunnel of red gates was behind her, and her mother and grandfather were gone. She peeked into the shrine grounds – they were empty. She stood there in the glowing red light, fear welling up in her stomach. She shouted their names and ran to the path and looked down the dizzying stone staircase. No-one.

Fishing boats were leaving the bay far below. The harbour loudspeakers were piping an announcement. She wondered if there was an air *raid. American bombs were dropping on cities far to the south, her own city. Where was her mother? Her grandfather? Her brother was away on the mainland, fighting for the Emperor. When the war finished, would they be re-united?*

She sat on the top step of the staircase and cried. She heard the cockroaches rustling behind her. They were rushing through the gates, over the stones. She folded her arms over her head and, helpless with terror, waiting for the insects to climb over her tiny body.

*   *   *

She awakes on her sofa at home. The sense of abandonment is overwhelming – for a minute or two she's still in the Northern village, her family gone forever. Gradually her waking life swims back inside her: the Giants lost the game. She had a rough night at work. Bean started shouting and skipped his bill. Did Kovacs get him? He wasn't home when she got back. She looks around for her mobile. There is a glass of orange juice on the lounge table. She must have dropped off as soon as she poured it.

The vivid events at the shrine fade slowly away. Her terror and longing were real – she can still feel them receding like an echo – but it was a dream. How do emotions generate so falsely? Is a whole world, a whole person, so easy to create and destroy? She checks her mail. Nothing from Kovacs, just a cascade of updates about the launch, and nothing more. What launch? Her eyes settle on the comb on the table, and she instantly recalls Bean's stories - his dead sister, him starting the war.

So that's where the bad dream came from. She recalls the old man's wrinkled face, the gaps between his teeth, his horrible outburst. She feels the sensation of cockroaches in her hair. She shouldn't have brought it home. She'd kept it out of the bin because she thought it might be worth something, and now it's invaded her dreams. She shivers and stares forlornly at the beautiful, tainted gift. What a horrible man. She remembers his eyes wandering across her skin, his clumsy, sleazy compliments. She fell asleep in his kimono too – she goes to remove it, and finds Kovacs lying on the bed in his underpants and socks.

"Oh!" She jumps. "I thought the house was empty."

"You were asleep when I got home." He is watching the TV without sound, smoking a cigarette. "You slept right through it."

"Through what?"

"The missile launches. Three of them. The North has pushed the button again. Didn't you hear the sound-trucks outside?"

"Oh!" She runs to the screen. "Are we OK?" She looks at the Prime Minister, the news ticker, the reporters' microphones.

"They went straight over us again. Crashed in the sea."

"We shouldn't be tolerating this." Her voice trembles.

"We are trying to get international support for an airstrike," Kovacs says.

"Good!" She spits, and loosens the thick sash around her waist. "If the bastards won't listen to reason." She pulls the sash free. It has stains from when the creep thumped the table and spilt the whisky. "I just had a weird dream," she tells him. "I was a little girl in the North, left behind after the war with my grandparents." She tosses the kimono in the corner. He watches the screen. Reporters are crowded outside embassies. "Trapped forever," she whispers. "It was so sad. I was so scared."

She goes over to him and wraps his arms around him.

"Don't worry," he starts stroking her hair. "We'll be alright. They can't hurt us."

"Did you catch Ambrose?"

"Who?"

"The old creep who skipped his bill. I sent you his ID. He abused me and broke a webscreen."

"Really?"

She sighs. "You said you'd run a scan or something."

"Oh yeah. I did. They'll catch him." The screen shows the rockets in the stratosphere, three pins with corona flares at the end. It looks like military footage, blurred and covered in data symbols.

"He said some strange things," she continues. "He said I lived behind a screen, that the government told us lies. Listen," she laughs, "he thinks he started the Patriotic War!"

"You wrote." He stares at the news. "I have to go in." He announces, running his hands over her hips, then softening his voice, "but I was hoping you'd wake up first."

She lies back, staring at the roof. " He had a sister in the North."

He stops stroking. "The old man?"

"He gave me her antique hair comb as a gift. I brought it back to show you."

"Why?" he grins. "To check for traces of DNA?"

She laughs. "No, for listening devices." She rolls toward him to tell him about the cockroaches but he opens her bra. Silently, she lets him touch her. He grabs the remote, turns up the volume, and as the room fills with political updates and bombers flying along the border, they begin to make love. As their gasps start to cut short she lets out a sob, a single one, for the little girl in her dream.

*   *   *

The blue trucks are waiting. They are lined up outside the orphanage with their big back doors open, red lights flashing on top. Today is her turn. She has seen her name on the notice-board. They come every year and take them for a health check. Nice doctors and nurses in green uniforms give them orange juice and put wires on their bodies and measure their fingers and toes. Their blood is taken. They wear headphones and look at pictures of animals and flowers while listening to strange sounds. They all fall asleep and wake up back at the orphanage.

When her grandmother died, the village leaders put her in the orphanage. The orphan nuns are kind. They have found her lots of friends. She is in all the sports teams and there is a big library where they learn to read and write and add. She has learned all the Dear Nation's songs and legends. She has learnt about the Committee and America and what to do if they drop a bomb. She has learnt to cook and sew. They have other lessons too – a Committee Member sometimes takes her to a building in the mountains above the town. He shows her movies of women making babies. They study lots of new words and talk for a long time. She always feels happy and peaceful afterwards. She is special. Everything is going to be OK. Soon there will be peace for everyone, he tells her, and she will find out what happened to her family.

She goes away in the blue ambulance. They change into their smocks and walk barefoot through the corridors of the clinic. This time they look between her legs where she's been bleeding recently. They paint red marks on her stomach. There are bright lights and they shave her head. Then she drinks the orange juice.

She awakes in a big dormitory. The bed is soft and comfortable, like the nuns' beds. She has cute pillows and fluffy sheets, unlike the orphanage. The room is full of older girls playing, talking, laughing. They all wear smocks of different colours. Some of them are fat with babies. They girls tell her she is

*beautiful. They have a wonderful meal together.
Afterwards the dear Committee Member is waiting
for her. She is so excited. He is wearing a blue
smock too. The doctor who is with him says they are
going to make a baby. She'll become like the happy
girls outside. The Dear Leader loves them, the
Committee Member said, and holds her very, very
close. The doctor is right - it doesn't hurt. They both
look her in the eyes and smile. She feels very special
and loved. Maybe the Committee Member is in love
with her. Maybe the Dear Leader too. As the man
moves quickly inside her, she looks up and she finds
herself staring into Kovacs' eyes, feeling Kovacs'
familiar body moving faster and faster...*

*   *   *

She suddenly awakes. Kovaks is gone; he has
reported to duty. His socks and underpants remain
on the bed and there is a semen stain on the quilt.
She immediately pulls the summer blue kimono off
the floor to cover her nakedness and for some reason
she remembers the Tanabata story, the magpie
bridge coming from the sky to hide the poor farmer
and his fairy bride. She still feels the doctor holding
her open, and the arms of the Committee Member
around her. Ambrose's childish stories. Why has she
dreamt of his sister again?

The TV blares. Animated rockets cross a google
map, trajectories ending harmlessly in the sea. The
commentary cuts to old interviews with Northern
abductees repatriated by the border raids. One's eyes

are blacked out. She is wearing the blue overalls of a Northerner. There are lines of semi-starvation on her face. They always show these documentaries when there is a new crisis with the North. But now it is like someone narrating her dream.

"There were lights outside my house, ambulance lights as if there'd been an accident. They carried me through the window. I wasn't sick. I awoke in a strange bed. There were rows of us there: young women of a certain genotype, they said. I could never think straight. They fed us strange coloured food. We kept having operations, and many fell pregnant. Sometimes girls were removed, and we never saw those girls again. The rumour was that their pregnancies were terminated. I had two babies there. I don't know what happened to them after they were born. We were told they would become Committee Members."

The interview jumps cuts, continues. "My third fetus was terminated. I was sent to the border, like all the failed mothers, to service the troops. Some of the boys were as young as ten. They said if we spent too long there we would end up servicing our sons. So I planned to escape…"

Saori blinks, confused. Is she still dreaming?

These escapee testimonies were used to justify the first border raids by Southern brigades, which repatriated dozens of Southerners. Some were slaves in factories and brothels, some were undergoing 'special education' in military and intelligence schools. Some were being trained as sleeper agents. Many claimed to have been abducted as children from coastal villages and ports. All over the country during the Partition, it transpired, Northern boats had pulled into remote bays and kidnapped children from the streets.

The world was outraged. Further Southern incursions led to occupied zones on the border, internationally approved. Crippling sanctions have been imposed. The world is now waiting for the belated collapse of the Northern regime. This latest stunt smacks of desperation. The presenter breaks for an ad.

A slick silver car drives through a wilderness, ploughing through rivers, up rocks, over green meadows. Saori finds the image comforting.

A life full of happiness inside
peaceful mother nature.
She drifts off to sleep.

*　　　*　　　*

Get up slowly." Kovacs is looking down at the wrinkled face of creature hiding in the forest. It's wearing a battered old top hat. He has his taser ready - his Safety Team partner is standing behind him on the shrine steps. A blimp reported a figure lurking in the Kirin Shrine forest. No-one is exempt from the curfew. The suspect rolls into a fetal position in the leaves, and squeezes its eyes tight. Kovacs grabs its elbow and drags it roughly upright. "What are you doing out here?" Its feet spin on the forest floor, and its walking stick waves around. Good Lord, its even wearing tails. Slowly the fool finds its feet and begins to brush its trousers free of leaves.

"Excuse me," the figure gasps. "I must have nodded off."

Red and blue lights circle on top of his sound truck, illuminating the walls of houses, the shrine gates, the trees.

"Nodded off? Have you been drinking?"

"I was visiting the shrine."

"At 1 AM? Do you understand you are concealing yourself during a curfew? Hold up your arms." He pats the skinny body down. He finds a webscreen remote control in a jacket pocket. Another contains a mobile phone. Both are broken. "What are these?"

"Things I picked up," it replies.

"Do you often carry trash around?" Kovacs keeps the devices in one hand and leads him out of the forest to his waiting team member. "Stay next to him. Let me check procedure," he sighs. He scrolls through a manual then recites: "are you in pain, or experiencing any discomfort or distress?"

"Not at all," the suspect grins. "Just a bit of apnea." He taps his head. "Too old you see. I was early for a meeting so I went for a stroll. I suppose the night air catches up on you."

"A meeting? With who?"

"With the Emperor."

His partner chuckles quietly. Kovacs sighs. They both relax the grips on their weapons. Kovacs holds out his hand. "ID." When the old man reaches into his breast pocket his walking stick slips and he stumbles onto one knee. Kovacs utters an expletive and grabs his arms again, dropping the consoles on the path. Still on one knee, the old man produces a card. As his partner helps him up, Kovacs swipes the card and they wait for the scan.

"Quite a long way from home, aren't we Professor?"

"Well, my appointment was interrupted by an air raid. I thought it best to take cover in the shrine grounds."

"Air raid…" His partner mutters. Kovacs continues reading from the manual.

"During public alerts citizens must take shelter in state-registered premises." The old man grins agreeably back.

His partner asks: "is it worth taking him to the lock up?"

"We're not taking him home. Throw him in the back."

The sound truck slides between the plasma screen billboards that line the road. The old nut is sitting quietly in the cage, grinning inanely, hands folded in his lap. Kovacs takes a gulp from his bucket of Cool Sweat and finds the right lane for the bridge. He can see the long arch in the distance. A blimp hovers over it, in red alert mode. Its motivational message slowly changes:

This Spectacle is Monopolised
While We Dream of Freedom.

That's an unusual one, he thinks, and chats to his partner. "How was your Tanabata?"

"Family picnic. Fireworks. Went home for the game."

"Giants fan?"

"Yeah."

"Too bad."

In his line of work he has found sports fanaticism to be an ideal mood regulator. It produces predictable stimulus / response patterns and creates politically inactive mass behaviour.

"Yeah, then this damn launch woke the kids up."

"Bastards. They know it's a festival day."

"I hope they bomb those launch pads flat."

"They will. A squadron of jets went over the border."

The blimp slowly drifts south, sucking in messages and transmitting the news. The car navigator is calling out directions. He monitors the office memo-stream across the dash, and updates his location status.

Their vehicle slides under neon signs, over complex underground machinery. He looks at the neon reflections on the surface of the truck making yellow blue waves, green circles, red squares as he drives. He looks at the live camera image on the screen - the same images are there – his sound truck racing through the streets, the Peach Boy logo painted on the side, the neon shapes swirling, he can even see himself in there, looking at the image transmitted by the street cameras he passes… he briefly wonders if there is really any difference between the images in his mind and those on the screen.

The screen images come from an electrical circuit of digital data, a stream of zeroes and ones, interpreted by a computer programme. The reality that he experiences comes from data in his senses, interpreted by cognitive networks in his brain. What do his senses actually perceive? A stream of zeroes and ones? Do his neural networks open some data and not others? Does some data need different programmes? In his line of work he often wonders such things.

"Officer Kovacs?"

"Yes?" Kovaks glances in the mirror and sees the suspect sitting in his top hat, holding his cane with a satisfied grin. No neural networks there. Is his operating programme corrupted? He shakes his head and takes a drink from the Cool Sweat bucket.

"Would you like to hear my version of the Tanabata story?" Did he give the suspect his name?

"Not just now," Kovacs replies.

"This bridge coming up – it was once a bridge of magpies, connecting the realm of the fairies to the realm of humans."

"Right. Thanks for that."

"Connecting imagination to reality. Mind to matter, light to darkness, the Earth to the stars. Like the human brain, Officer Kovacs."

His partner laughs. "Well, it's not a human brain is it, mister. It's a concrete bridge."

"And the fairy is a dwarf."

Kovacs stays silent, and pulls onto the bridge.

"Seriously, Officers. Altair, the star that represents the fairy in the Tanabata story? It's actually a white dwarf."

"Do I need to know that?" Kovacs asks.

"The farmer in the story is Vega, and twelve thousand years ago, when farming first began, Vega was the pole star."

"The what?" His partner asks.

"The star around which all the others spin. But the earth wobbles in its orbit," the crazy professor is now spinning one finger around another, "which changes the relative position of the stars."

Kovacs tries to ignore him. He's still thinking: which car is the real car? The one passing through his senses, or the one on his screen? In each image, he is inside the car - is he then just an image inside his own mind? If so, is his mind his? This is an important question, in his line of work.

The suspect has pressed his wrinkled face into the grille separating them. "It also changes the order of the years." Kovacs sighs and looks out the window. The billboards are reflected in the river below the bridge. A model's perfect face has fallen into the water, and is floating and coming apart. Fireflies are looping slowly on the banks and there are people running around down there, clutching sparklers. That's a breach of curfew. A firework arcs into the sky and explodes. He presses an alarm button on his screen, and circles its location.

"Do you know what year it is now?" The fool carries on. They are five minutes away and Kovacs decides to humour him. "I believe it's the year of the mouse, Professor." He says officiously.

"Oh no its not." Bits of spittle are flying from his mouth as he speaks. "Because of the precessionary wobble the calendars are wrong. It's not the year of the mouse at all."

"Let's hope it's the year of the Giants then!" His partner jokes.

Bony fingers grip the grille. "No, not that either. It's the year of man!"

"What?" Kovacs jerks around to face his captive, but he's not there. He hits the brakes. He grabs his taser and shoves it through the bars. "Sit up!" He orders. There is no movement. "Where is he?" He barks orders at his partner, leaps out and throws open the backdoor. The cage is empty.

They run along the bridge, shining their torches in the drains. There's nobody moving on the empty road. He shouts at his partner: "He may have jumped!" They peer over the bridge. The people below seem to have suddenly left. He could throw a cordon around the area, conduct a proper search. He hesitates, weighing options. The billboard screen changes. Now images of fast food images float in the water. Kovacs looks up and sees the stars glowing high above. "What did he say before he disappeared, do you recall?"

His partner stares at him in a puzzled way. "Er, something about a pole star?"

"After that. When he was talking about what year it was."

"Oh, the year of man," his partner recalls, "or something like that."

"I thought so." He rummages through the car - the broken consoles, the phone, the remote, what happened to them? Finding nothing, he finally

remembers the first crazy thing the Professor said –
a meeting with the Emperor – and slaps his face
hard. He grabs his phone and scrolls the evening's
update threads. Saori's: *he's wearing tails would you
believe?* How could he be so stupid? He dials her
number.

*   *   *

*She had arrived in the South wanting to wear nice
kimonos again, like the ones she had before the war,
but she was still in her overalls. Through the big
window she could see the freeways and parks, the
powerful cars and silver trains, but she sat on a bed
in a small room. Glassed apartment buildings
reflected the sky. Her bathroom was tiled and the
taps ran hot and cold. The webscreen on the wall
was a display of wealth – sitcoms set in wide
apartments, actors in beautiful dresses, busy streets
glittering with commerce, police and villains
fighting with hi-tech gadgets. The rumours had been
true: the South really was richer than the North.*

*They said she was still in 'quarantine'. They said
her blue overalls were part of her identity. She had
to be de-programmed and it had to happen slowly.
Her false worldview must be carefully
deconstructed. She would be allowed to leave soon.
They would give her a new name and new money
and a steady job. They would raise her in a safe
house until she was just like every other citizen.*

*There was a knock on the door and Kovacs came
in. He kissed her. He was her guide through this*

strange landscape of fact and fiction. He knew how to prune and nurture her delicate psyche and regrow a complete person. She opened her mouth to his, and their desire replaced the feelings of disappointment. They said falling in love with him was a natural part of the process. A genuine adult relationship would heal the betrayed child within. She would learn the compassion and care of her new society, and achieve psychic reintegration

He poured her a glass of orange juice. She drank it and lay down. He sat by the window and read the newspaper while she prepared. Then he stood. Today was a new stage in the process, he said. They had to go deeper into the fictions she had grown up with. There were further layers of illusion to strip away.

"I want you to go back to that first day in the North, when you visited the shrine at your grandparents' village," Kovacs said .

She felt an old fear return: the cockroaches swarming, the fear of abandonment. Why had there been no goodbye? How had she got down the mountain alone?These were the questions. After the cockroaches fell from the shrine roof, her mother wiped her face with a handkerchief; the memory included the intimate smell of spittle on white cloth.

"We believe some of those memories may be false," he said. "There are discontinuities and some missing time."

False? An empty space yawned in her stomach. The combination of the medicine and these words made her feel nauseous, like she was standing on a precipice in her mind. She remembered looking down the stone steps at the fishing boats in the bay far below. She could hear the outboard engines throttling, the captain's radio chattering. Behind her the cockroaches rushed through the trees toward her back. Her skin shivered involuntarily. They were going to swamp her, crawl in her mouth.

"The detail of the cockroaches seems fantastical," his voice continued. "You talk of them so credulously yet have you ever see such a thing before or since? Such phenomena are indications of neural tampering."

The ship captain's radio? Previously she'd heard loudspeakers on the wharf, and feared it was an air raid. She shouldn't be able to hear a ship radio from a mountaintop. The memory had changed. She looked down the cliff, a dizzying slope to the water far below, and leapt from the top of the steps. The trees, the steps, the blue bay spun in her head. The mountainside was steep and she flew a long way through the air before she hit the forest floor. She cartwheeled through a small landslide of loose earth and leaves. It was in her hair and mouth and clothes.

As she slid down the mountainside, she realised that she had a life jacket on. With a dizzying rush she realised: she had never climbed the mountain at all. She had been on the boat. She was in a fishing trawler with a firm male hand holding her into her seat. She couldn't breathe. Her mother was running along the distant wharf, screaming. She begins screaming too.

Kovacs brings her back, and holds her as she shivers. "You see Saori, the memories were implanted to occlude your abduction. They isolated that memory and planted novel suggestions in it, which your brain, desperate for order and continuity, wove seamlessly into your reality. But now we have found the anomalies and fantastic content which prove those memories to be as thin and weak as paper plastered over cracks in a wall."

A group of men were holding her mother on the dock. She was hysterical, trying to leap into the water. The ship engines roared and lifted the bow out of the flat blue water. The captain's radio chattered urgent instructions. Northern agents were taking her away. They had stolen her.

*   *   *

She awakes in the fetal position, sobbing, her arms tied up inside a life-jacket… no, they are tied up inside the blue kimono, which has wrapped around her as she slept. The fluorescent light is still on. The TV is blaring loudly. She is tangled in the silken folds. She experiences the horrible sensation that she is falling asleep as she awakes. The kidnapped child inside her, like a forgotten memory, is now being snuffed out as she kicks and struggles. Everything she looks at – the furniture, her room, the TV, the mundane objects on her dresser - all hint at another dimension looming beneath. She gets the impression the material world is just a reflection of images on the surface of a sphere. She feels that the person inhabiting the room is a shallow reflection of a far richer being within; Saori is a thin layer of thoughts and memories describing someone much larger and more complete.

The other girl inside her is disappearing into incoherent thought. She pulls herself free of the kimono and lies there panting, exposed to the white fluorescence of the room. Just a dream.

On the TV is the same advertisement that was on before: a large 4WD with blacked-out windows is driving over rocks and rapids. With perfect smoothness it runs through alpine wilderness with a tableau of snowy peaks in the background. Perhaps she has only been asleep a few seconds. She notices the car has a Peach Boy logo on its door, a strange example of cross-advertising. Classical music swells on the soundtrack. The image suggests perfect, unrestricted freedom. The car drives onto a sheer cliff, approaches the sheer edge, and doesn't stop – it drives straight over and drops out of shot. Her hand goes to her mouth. A slogan runs across the screen:

What kind of dream do you watch?

Change heart of deep world.

Her heart skips. The car's sickening fall feels, in her stomach, like her dream when she jumped from the steps. She picks up the remote and flicks through the channels. She finds the Giants game, stops to watch but remembers they lost and continues flicking and finds the car ad again. Classical music swells. It drives onto the cliff. She checks if it goes over again. It does. She calls out in disbelief and flicks, looking for news, but there's just car, football, car, football, car, football.

Then the car ad changes. The black Peach Boy utility is back in the city. There are no glass high rise, no billboards, the rooves are unfinished: it looks like the Occupied Zone. The car is dodging piles of burning rubbish scattered between the buildings. With optimum power steering it swings around potholes. Masked youths run from street corners, there is a hip-hop soundtrack:

Step into the new and we will
fill the gap in your heart.

As the wheels spin pass, the camera lingers on a close-up of broken glass and blood-splattered shoes. Then with precision suspension the wheels run over the attached legs of a streetfighter.

She doesn't understand this. She changes channel, and finally there is a newscast. Helicopters are launching rockets into a war zone city. The camera is hand-held, running at street level. There is pandemonium, smoke, blood, rubble. Northern characters appear and disappear on the screen. The wobbling lens zooms onto the helicopter. Another rocket deposits a plume of white smoke above the city. Saori can make out the unmistakeable shape of a Big Ears surveillance system on it. Is this a live feed?

Hands shaking, she again changes channel. The wheels operate under individualized torque-saving microchips, withdrawing independently inside the chassis. The bodies roll and scatter on the road, bones and joints fluid. Peach Boy runs along behind, an animated figure imposed on the footage. The hip-hop is smooth and uninterrupted.

Listen to his happy smile!

What kind of world do you watch?

Again, the observable world around her seems to be cast on a brittle surface, the papering-over of vast emptiness. Her phone rings. She snatches it – its Kovacs.

"What's happening?"

"I'm at work. Look, that old man at work you mention..."

"There's this weird stuff on TV," she sobs. "It's scary."

"Weird stuff? What do you mean?"

"There are helicopters bombing a city. And the car ads are running over dead bodies …"

"Car ads? Bodies?"

"I've been dreaming a lot tonight. They won't stop." She chokes a little "The car ads won't stop."

"Slow down, sweetie. Everything's fine."

The webscreen is showing armed men running down a street, against a tide of people going the other way in makeshift masks, carrying stretchers. A crowd is mobbing the black Peach Boy utility – it falls on its side. Is this smuggled footage?

"Honey there's violent footage on TV. Like propaganda from over the border. Are we at war?" She whispers. A crackle. She hears the hiss of space, like satellites in her earpiece. When he comes back on, his voice seems fainter.

"Look just turn the webscreen off OK?"

"OK." She doesn't. "Kovacs?"

"Yes?"

"I dreamed I was an abductee from the North. You were re-programming me."

There's a long silence on the phone.

"And now this stuff on TV. Kovacs, Big Ears is painted on the helicopters… the helicopters are bombing the citizens…"

"Forget about your dreams, Saori. Tell me. The guy that came into work…"

"Am I dreaming now?"

"Shut up! Concentrate. The one you complained about, the one who broke the remote or something. Can you describe him?"

She remembers the moment with a sickly taste. "Ambrose?" She feels dizzy.

"His name is not Ambrose. What did he look like?"

Saori's thoughts are grinding. Kovacs' voice keeps on going but she's not listening. She's looking at the gunships firing again and again into the city streets, as if a video game is replaying. *His name is not Ambrose. Yes, of course.* The phosphorous plumes drift and collapse like towers of white tissue. Women run past the camera, carrying children screaming from burn wounds. *I know who he is.*

"…Saori, what did he look like? Do you remember?"

"Of course I remember." She can see him, as clear as day, sitting on the floor of the private room, the broken remote next to him. "Just an ugly old man, you know. Balding. Missing teeth. Oh, and he was wearing tails, those old-fashioned clothes that the Emperor wears. Just a really weird guy."

"That's him." She can see him as if its not a memory at all, but a scene in front of her.

"Who is he?" She asks, knowing exactly who he is.

"I'll tell you later. Now, I left out some fresh orange juice. Drink it and go to sleep, OK?"

She sees the phone smashed on the floor, the young man storming out, leaving his undrunk bucket of Cool Sweat. She sees Ambrose in the Willow Room, hurling the remote at the webscreen, and she knows exactly what she has to do. She carries the phone into the lounge and sees the turtle-shell comb on the table, next to a tall glass of orange juice. The remembers its claw-like grip in her hair, feels the sensation of cockroaches on her skin. She remembers she dreamt this was a false memory. She picks up the orange juice and pours it onto the carpet. The line is still open.

"Kovacs?"

"Yes."

"Is that really you?"

"What?"

She picks up the comb and slides it into her hair. It grips.

"I don't think his sister was kidnapped at all."

"Saori you are not making sense. They are just dreams, honey. The terrorism is affecting your mind."

"No, I think I've been dreaming of something else all along. " She looks at the slogan on the screen, flashing now, over and over. "Kovacs?"

"I'm still here."

"You were right about the false memories."

"Look, its really important now that you just go back to sleep."

"No. I know what you've been trying to do. Has it been helping?"

"Helping? Sit down Saori. Have a drink. Rest. I'll come home soon."

"I have to go out now. I've been resting in this apartment too long."

"No! There's still curfew!"

"Don't worry. I will be fine. You'll see."

She shuts the phone, loosely ties up the wrinkled kimono, walks to the front door, slips on her shoes and goes out.

*   *   *

Kovacs is left standing next to the Safety Patrol van, staring at the disconnection icon on his mobile screen. He scrolls through his address book and makes another three calls, but there are no answers.

"Girlfriend trouble?" His partner is grinning cheekily at him. He smiles back sheepishly. "Yeah, she's a bit highly strung. Gets a bit nervous in these alerts."

She tilts her head sympathetically. "If you wanna go and check on her it's OK. I won't tell."

He looks at her. "You know, that's a good idea." He climbs into the passenger seat. "First we better put a section D out on that old man." He picks up the car-phone and calls central command. "Suspect escaped custody. ID reported. Last seen in the vicinity of Kirin Shrine. Wearing black tails and a top hat. No belt, no shoes. Extremely dangerous."

"Extremely dangerous? You serious?"

He smiles reassuringly. "I dunno. I just want him found. You can't just disappear from my truck without me knowing." He throws her the keys. "I'll catch up with you later. Thanks."

"You don't want a lift?"

"She doesn't live far. Just round the corner."

The electric engine hums and she drives off slowly, the rooftop speakers pealing soft advice. "*All citizens remain indoors! Safety Offices are securing the City.*"

He speed dials his region commander. "Boss, number 31 is experiencing mnemonic dilution. 33 and 36 are not answering … Are there any anamolous reports ? … I'm going to see her…. Got it. … Let the other aides know… I will."

He's already jogging towards Saori's apartment. He hangs up and runs as hard as he can.

*   *   *

She sees herself in the window of an empty shop front. In her kimono, clogs and comb she looks like a figure from the last century. She stops and looks up at the sky: dozens of aircraft circle above like fireflies. A river of stars arches overhead. She once learnt that looking at space was the same as looking at time.

Looking back at her historical image in the window, she realises she's been looking at the world the wrong way all her life. She's been experiencing it as fragments when in fact it is all joined up. She has understood her society as a whole lot of separate lives and experiences when in fact it is really just one single experience. The present moment is like a puzzle she played with as a child, made of different lines and colours which, when twisted and turned in the right way, resolved into a clear image. Her life up to now has been a scrawl of lines and colours, which now, with one twist, have all joined up into a pattern that is not her life at all.

Above her, Altair and Vega are embracing. Milky tears are dripping down her face. It's Tanabata and they are happy. The light shining from the lovers is two moments drawn through time and space to become one, blended and scattered through the atmosphere into a gentle shower of particles. It may be a dream, but she is happy too.

She steps down from the road and begins to walk across an empty field. Her thick wooden clogs sink into the mud, but her feet remain dry. A sound truck tinkles in the distance, its insistent, paranoid song. The streets are eerily empty, the traffic lights flashing orange, except for a lone figure sprinting along a distant stretch. She realises, with some detachment, it's probably Kovacs. She pauses: she is just a shadow to him. He has no idea of her true identity, nor she of his. They are not yet aware of the object they are part of. Maybe he soon will be, maybe not. She can only know her own part in this, yet clearly their fates are entangled. She'd better hurry.

*   *   *

Because of the curfew there is a lock-in at the nearby bar, and the shoes of revelers are piled up at he door. I find a pair of slip-ons that almost fits and sneak around the building. The red lanterns glowing outside indicate the dishes on offer, and the ages, weights and hair styles of the girls serving them. The roar of gorging arises from within, mixed with the wails of popular songs. Hot steam is blowing out of the air conditioning vents, covering me in rich kitchen smells as I wait in some rice fields behind the bar. The fields are abandoned, hemmed in by suburban houses. Inside the curtained windows, people's shadows cross before the blue flicker of screens. They are having a restless, anxious night: jet fighters are circling the city. Airships are rattling above buildings, sucking up their voices, keystrokes and secrets; regurgitating news updates and slogans. We are safe, we are protected, we are busy with our wishes and their brief satisfaction. We are provided with interesting toys and entertainments. We are absorbed by the sensory world inside our own heads, building a fine palace for our identities, with high walls and fortressed turrets. At the centre of it all, the Emperor is asleep, sweating, fearful. But it will soon be time to awake.

Here she comes, stepping carefully through the field like a farm girl from one hundred years ago. I stand as best I can but have to hold up my trousers – I got new shoes, but my belt is still back in custody. She looks up at me smiling, her face bathed in starlight and invisible waves of information. She has the turtle-shell comb in her hair.

She points up into the sky – three bright new stars are crossing. The launched satellites have reached orbit and are beginning to circle the globe, bathing it in new data. No doubt the Big Ears blimps are trying to repair this breach of wall security, scramble it back into lines and shapes, zeroes and ones. They are already reporting that the rockets have crashed into the sea. Most citizens will believe this, not bothering to use their own eyes.

She pats the pockets of my tails and finds the consoles there. I lift them out and her smile breaks into a grin. Like the gentleman I am, I spread my tails over the muddy grass, and she kneels gracefully with the instruments in her lap. She inspects the broken phone, taps the intact screen. She grabs the smashed remote control, turns it over, checks the loose wires and the batteries. She takes the comb from her hair, uses it to unscrew the back covers and inserts one tooth into a port in the phone; it lights up brightly. Mei Lee's comb seems to be full of internal tools, diodes and circuits.

I rub my hands in glee. I had a hunch the consoles would come in useful. For her, its obvious that these two broken pieces of junk are neither broken nor separate; they are simply not connected up properly. She exposes the circuit boards of each appliance and starts soldering them together with another of the comb's teeth. Her fingers are in a flurry. I feel delighted to find myself playing a tiny and ignorant part in some larger plan. My personal madness has proven to have an impersonal method.

Within minutes she is finished. The screen flickers and glows. She holds the whole assembly in one hand and reaches out to me with the other. Planting my cane in the mud, I pull her up and we stand in the field. One Northern satellite is crossing the centre of the sky, outshining the Tanabata stars, which have reached the zenith. The other two satellites have changed trajectory, and are bending across the night sky. She holds the contraption up: framed by the summer triangle, the screen covers the bulging glow of the galaxy's centre. Still holding up my trousers, I grip her hand and the scar around my heart glows. I feel like we are standing between two countries, tied to each other, to myth and to history.

The buttons flicker as if something is being uploaded. Surrounding her hand are the galaxy's vast dust lanes and nebulae, like distant flocks of birds teeming towards us. Is Saori's new contraption a bridge to the satellites above and the cosmos beyond? We are not two people but one compound being of matter, time and light, carried by thought, refracted by the past, reflecting off the mirrors between nations, reaching this point here, on this one night, a chance perspective, an orbital parallax – two stars becoming one.

The screen in Saori's hand flickers into an image: a woman in a cosmonaut's suit, with her helmet off. She is floating, weightless. Her blonde hair is drifting around her head. The picture is glitchy, lined with flickering numbers and icons; her eyes are directed to the left of the camera, perhaps looking at the same data. As she waits, she reaches behind her head and pins back her weightless blonde hair with a large turtle-shell comb. Then she turns to the screen and nods professionally, like a news reader. Some icons at the bottom of the screen flash and she breaks into a celebratory smile.

The diodes within Saori's comb begin to glow. A data counter at the bottom of the screen begins to fill with some information. The cosmonaut shuffles some papers in front of her and begins to read. Saori thumbs the plastic volume button and a tiny static voice emerges.

The Cosmonaut's Tale

"In the centre of the town where my grandfather grew up there was an old clocktower, curving sharply from its base like a fish tail. It was made of wood, like all the buildings in the town, and its clock faces reared high above all the houses. By the time my grandfather was born, the clock had long ceased working. The hands always read half past six, as they had broken and swung to the bottom of their arc. Yet it had once been vital to village life, telling workers in the fields when to stop digging or planting, or when to break for lunch, or when the sick should be fed and the children collected from school. Some said it was thousands of years old. Some said it was more ancient than that. An old legend said that the clocks had been built by an ancient group of people who used to wander from village to village. These men and women wore black clothes and green hats, and taught many wondrous things such as the properties of circles and springs, and how to find water and bend wood, and where to build a church, and the angles between the stars, and – obviously - how to tell the time.

My grandfather was told they would visit once a year and hold up geometrical instruments to the sky, and sometimes make tiny adjustments to the hands of the clock – forward a minute or two, backward a few seconds. Time was of utmost import, they said, because the clocktower was our connection to the sun and the moon, and our lifeline to the stars and the heavenly bodies, and should this connection go adrift the village would get out of harmony with the heavens, and the crops wouldn't grow, and the animals would give birth at the wrong time, and everyone would starve. Each year after setting the clock they would wander through the town asking for offerings from door to door, then move on to the next village over the mountains.

"So people gave them offerings, and worked and planted and slept according to the time and instructions given, and let these scientists maintain the clock, and for a long time no-one starved at all.

"Then came the year the sun began to change. It stopped rising at the usual time, and set in strange places – sometimes on one side of the mountain, some days the other, some days across the lake, or at times well before the clock said it should. People at first thought the clock had simply broken a spring or a hand, or that others had forgotten where the sun usually set, and so carried on planting and irrigating the fields, and feeding the sick and sending the kids to school. Whatever was going on, they were certain that soon the scientists would come and fix it.

"But sometimes the school children found themselves walking home in the dark, or the shadows would stretch across the fields in the wrong direction. One week the soil suddenly heated so the flowers withered, the next it cooled so the seeds died, and the villagers realised the clock alone couldn't do this, and began to fear. Had their village fallen out of harmony with the heavens? Were the scientists' settings and calculations wrong? They sent an urgent message for them to come straight away, but before the messenger returned two terrible things happened.

"First, a goat was born from a sheep. The whole village came to see it. They filed past the copper box where it was kept, for neither it nor its mother could touch the ground, and threw salt on the unnatural pair. Then a boy fell into a fit-like sleep, and was also put into a copper cot, and the villagers stared in horror at his body staying rigid and tight, while white foam rose from his mouth. His eyes stayed tightly closed, but moved erratically beneath the lids as if he were dreaming.

The village opinion was that both omens were caused by the same forces that had changed the sun – but whether it was a balancing force trying to break into the disturbed world with a message of how to set it right, or the disturbance itself growing stronger and more ominous, was a point of constant argument. Some pointed at the sky, sure they had seen the sun revolving in circles, others made marks on sundials that proved the sun's movements were within normal parameters, while others said that these things happened every year, it was just that no-one had ever noticed them before. Then the messenger returned and threw things further into confusion: all the clocks in all the villages had broken, he reported, and all the days everywhere were out of tune with eachother, and the scientists were frantically trying to fix the clocks and take measurements. They told him they would come as quickly as they could, and added the village's name to the bottom of a list.

"The village elders decided to take matters into their own hands. They had no need for the scientists to tell them that the sun was rising lower and lower each day. By now anyone could observe it: every morning it crawled into the sky over the mountain tops, then it seemed to stay motionless amongst the peaks for an hour or two. It then zig-zagged across the horizon before falling into the valley, turning the river an unworldly shade of yellow. Other strange events happened - one day, butterflies flew down from the mountain slopes and gathered inside the cupboards in the houses, seeking out plates bearing pictures of flowers. Trees began raising their roots through floorboards. One week the lake emptied and in the next the wells overflowed.

The harvests were late; the crops either flowered early or didn't set seed. Some were eaten by swarms of pests. The elders ran cattle between fires, and burnt effigies of mice and foxes and other creatures of fertility, but the crop-shoots remained low and pale, and the bees sleepy. They decided to sacrifice sheep in the fields, to encourage them to harvest sooner. Throats were bled into the soil, liberating pure life from the body, but the sun stayed still, and the river reduced to a trickle. The ewe-born goat was next – this was burnt alive in a pyre, but the fruit stayed green on the trees, and a few days later it began to snow. It had never snowed before, but instead of joy and wonder, there was only cold and fear - and the desperate chopping of fruit trees and furniture. The snow didn't stop. The villagers awoke on the seventh day of the blizzard to find wolves chasing reindeer through the streets. Enraged and terrified, the villagers carried the fitful boy and his mother outside, raised a scaffold on the clocktower, and bound the two of them to it – they planned to burn them both. Some of the elders tried to stop this, saying the boy must be preserved so the scientists could inspect him, but other elders were leading the mob, and it was only the sudden and serendipitous appearance of one scientist – an old, tired-looking woman with grey hair under her crumpled green hat – that silenced them. Dismounting from her horse, she drew a dagger out of her frayed black cloak and, saying nothing, marched through the stunned crowd and cut the unconscious boy and woman down, and kicked at the scaffold base so that it fell.

"With a despairing look on her face, and without asking for permission or even an explanation, she carried the boy to an open sleigh behind her horse, threw him in, and rode north out of town. People peered into the sleigh as it left – there were a dozen other children asleep in there, wrapped up in sacks; round-eyed, square-eyed, blue-haired, yellow-haired, black-skinned, red-skinned children of every type in the world, all drooling and fitful, suffering the same sickness as our boy. As she reached the village gates she hesitated, stopped, drove back and hired the messenger she had met previously to accompany her. Then she continued on.

"They drove north through the snow and mountains. The messenger cooked and cleaned for the woman, and ensured the children didn't get cold, and helped lift the sleigh when it became stuck in snow-drifts or risked the icy slopes. The sun rose lower and lower in the sky every day, growing dimmer and redder. It seemed the world was becoming a mesh of shadows – shadows of trees within shadows of mountains within the shadow of the earth itself. The moon rose in strange places, the stars swirled in their spheres – had the Earth been unleashed from its orbit? After a week they came out of the mountains onto a huge white plain stretching into the distance. The plain was dotted with thin forests and covered with reindeer numbering in the millions. Moving in and out of the herd, in their hats and cloaks and sleds, were hundreds of scientists, hunting the reindeer and collecting the mushrooms which were the only thing left growing in the forests. The messenger said later that the woman smiled for the first time since they had left our village, and emitted a loud and high holler.

"As they heard the woman's cry, the scientists ran up to her with great excitement, and stared into the back of the sleigh to inspect the sleeping children. One by one the scientists picked them gently up and carried them to one of the many cone-shaped tents that were scattered across the plain, each one trailing a brown column of smoke from the top. To the messenger's astonishment, they did not enter through the wall but carried the children straight up the pine struts on the outside of the hides, and lowered them down through the smoke-hole at the top. Once they had all the sleeping children inside the tent, they immediately began a great feast. They had stockpiled reindeer meat and mushrooms inside the tent, and they played music, sang and danced to drums for what seemed like days, while the children lay on their cots, twitching and fitting and frothing at the mouth. The scene was so intoxicating that soon our messenger forgot the cold outside, and the bitter wilderness, and the uncanny fears raised by the strange behaviour of the sun and the scientists and the children.

"Once, waking from a sleep he had forgot he fell into, he went outside and there was complete darkness. He felt a lonely, terrifying absence. The sun was gone. It had completely and finally abandoned the sky and earth. Bitter winds blew through the icy pine trees. He felt that the world was dying. Wolves were howling and dying, the children were crying, the pine trees were dying and he would die, yet the stupid scientists inside the tents were unable to do anything about it. Their feast continued, and the music played on - drums thumping and bells ringing, dancers flickering on the walls - but all seemed doomed. Some vital cosmic connection had broken and the sun had spun away from the Earth and sky. The tents and the plain and the mountains and villages and rivers and clocktowers would be buried in black cosmic dust forever.

"The Sun is dead!" he lamented, running between the tents. "The Sun is dead!" He ran through the scientists' settlement panicking and shouting, banging on the hides and flaps to interrupt the pitiful denial going on inside.

"But the drums only beat louder. The bells and cymbals intensified their rhythms. Only one figure appeared – the old woman who had employed him from the village. She shook her long grey hair out of her green hat, and stood in the snow and held her arms aloft to the inky sky.

"What are you doing now?" He demanded. "Praying to these cold stars? Commanding the sun to fly back into your arms?"

"No. I'm taking measurements." She replied.

"Your numbers are still going to save us? Your equations and instruments are going to bring everything back to life again?" The messenger wept with fear and anger. "They are useless! They have done nothing to stop this happening. You are powerless! All along you have tricked us out of alms and offerings with your fake knowledge. And now we are falling through space and time, lost and frozen."

"She turned to him with a calm smile. "You are right." She told him. "The sun has died. It is buried in the coffin of the earth, so we are playing its funeral rites. But look!" She raised her hands to the sky again. "The light of all other suns shines on and on forever. Life and light is eternal. How can this be? Look at the laws of the universe – nothing is forever, yet nothing truly disappears either, it only moves and transforms from one state to another. Does one broken heart mean all the love in the world is over? When one ruler dies is that the end of the nation? No, his child inherits the crown, and new lovers embrace. When the grain is cut, or the calf killed, do all beings die? On the contrary, their bodies renew from the seeds and bones of others. This process is eternal, but how can you see it if you are fixed on a your own fickle love, your own temporary rule, your own single body? Watch with us, and wait: you will see a new sun arise from its earthly coffin, just as certainly as love returns to a broken heart. You will see that all beings can awake to eternal life. It may seem mysterious but it is not. It is the same process written into the tablet of time and space. It is not our numbers and measurements, or our beliefs, that make it so, but the natural law on which numbers are based. Just as a new sun will be born from the heavens, so these children will rise up from their fit, and return with you to their villages, to bring new life and a new epoch. This is what we expect. You do not have to trust us, but just settle down and wait, and you may witness a miracle."

"The old woman went back inside her tent, and picked her drum back up, but the messenger shook his head, refusing to believe a word of what she had said. He sat in the snow staring into the dark night, which is exactly what she had asked him to do.

As he sat in despair, as the night grew blacker and the stars shone brighter and colder, the icicles lengthened into claw shapes by the grip of night. The air grew so frigid that the messenger's jacket cracked open, and shards fell from his beard, but he refused to go back inside the tents – he would die in reality, not in denial or blind faith. After a time, the drumming fell silent. The fires died, deepening the darkness. A deadly silence stretched across the plain.

The scientists filed out of the tents, slowly and sadly, and sat in the snow with him, hanging their heads. The messenger realised the scientists had given up. They had realised the folly of their ways.

"The messenger stood wearily, and gathered his strength for one last act on the dying Earth. They had left the children in the tent, to freeze to death alone. For what it was worth, he would help them. He opened up the flap of the tent, and recoiled in shock. All the children were sitting upright, eyes wide open, staring upwards at the cone of the tent. They slowly walked in line to the poles, grasped them and began to climb. First one reached the cone in the roof and disappeared through it, then another, and another. As the fourth one left the tent, the messenger saw its hair light up with a golden halo of light.

"A huge cheer rose up. The messenger ran outside and beheld a wondrous sight: the children were standing on the roof of the tent, bathing in rays of sunlight. The tip of a giant globe was grazing the southern sky, shedding golden light across the plain, onto the tops of the trees, and the tents, and the faces of the children as they climbed dòwn the outside, smiling and crying.

"The scientists too were weeping joyously, hugging each other and rejoicing. The messenger joined them. The old woman had been right. They had solved the mystery of the dying sun and the sleeping children, and the Earth was going to live again.

But the scientists did not return. They could have trumpeted their mastery of number, returned their children to their parents and paraded in triumph through the villages. But they didn't. They just sent the messenger back with the children in the sleigh through the melting ice of the plains and the mountains, and he received all the joy and wonder of the celebrating populace. As for the scientists, they were never seen again.

"Only the children remain as their legacy. These children still wander from village to village like the scientists did, but without knowing how to fix the clocks or repair the clocktowers. They have another purpose: for every year now when the snow flies and the sun sinks low, they disappear in their sleighs to the great northern plain where the sun sleeps in its earthly coffin, and there they wait in the darkness for three days, singing and feasting, and then return to the villages, climbing down the chimneys of every house with gifts of meat and sweets for the villagers, and the message: you too can awake! Arise! Awake to eternal life!"

*   *   *

Framed between the Tanabata stars, the woman on the screen begins to flicker and snow. She smiles off-camera for a brief flash, as if she has completed a long and exhausting trial, and then her face is cut by jagged lines of interference. The satellite is dropping below the horizon, all three are beaming messages into other nations.

Saori inspects her device, then straps the phone back to back to the remote control with a wrist band. I pick up my now muddy tails and top hat, don them as best I can, and reach for her hand, but she's scrolling through her work, picking menus and options.

"What you told me tonight is true," she says as she thumbs. "I've always felt I've been living behind a screen, and parts of me have been kept out of view."

"Yes. We've been living in a labyrinth built around the truth," I reply, "in our personal lives and in our civilisation, for centuries."

"Whole parts of me have been living on the other side of a border, a border we never think about. The person I call me on this side is completely manufactured, a character conjured out of fragments, half-remembered lives and imagined histories, like a person in a dream."

"We think we are approaching the centre of the labyrinth, not realising the paths are always leading away."

She shows me the screen, which is now replaying the cosmonaut's tale. "This is the message launched over us tonight: don't stay on the path. Go over the walls." She walks toward the nearest dwelling, smiling back over her shoulder. "What do you think is at the centre of the labyrinth?"

"The Emperor, asleep on his throne." I answer, trying to catch her up, but she gets to the wall, grabs onto a downpipe and starts climbing. She knows I can't follow her. I can see her handprints and footprints on the pipe as she scrambles over the ledge onto the tiles. "I'll see you at the palace," she calls back, climbing the apex of someone's roof, the blue-ray light in the bound handset flickering brightly. "You go up the alleys, while I go down the chimneys."

Saori points her handset into the small metal chimney on the roof. No doubt the webscreens in the house will flicker and snow, then resolve into an image of the cosmonaut in her satellite, turning to the camera, shuffling her papers, beginning to read. Saori jumps airily to the next roof, lands safely, and waves to me. I wave back, and head for the alley.

A flickering blue line cuts from her handset across the field, zig-zagging through the air, hitting the microwave relay station, outlining the airship's oval bulk behind it The dishes blow out in showers of sparks. The airship yawls, adrift, screen flickering and snowing. Explosions rock the air and our journey back to the centre begins, Saori walking over the rooves, me slinking under them. In the distance, another blimp flames to the ground. She has a city to awake, and I an appointment to keep.

The Imperial Palace

Kovacs jumps through the open door of Saori's apartment and strides through every room, throwing open wardrobes and checking behind doors. His boots leave a trail of sand and debris – he didn't bother with this courtesy. The webscreen is still on in the bedroom, his underwear is rumpled on the bed, but Saori is gone.

Kovacs is stunned. The screen shows helicopter gunships hovering over a Northern border town. The footage is taken from street-level, where people are gathered behind walls, some in uniform, others in casual clothes. The gunships are gutting a government building with heavy fire. People are piling bodies into flatbed cars and putting out fires with buckets. There is a date flashing on the screen – a few days before – and a location: an occupied town sealed off from the South by the Border Protection Wall. It is the same town where he repatriated Saori in a factory raid ten years ago, before he quit the Special Forces and joined the de-programming unit.

The street footage is obviously filmed by Northerners; Kovacs is wondering how the hell it has got onto the network. Southern citizens never see these attacks, They only know the Occupied Zones as a source of 'sleepwalkers': mind-controlled Northeners sent over the border, strapped to bombs.

The gunships, clearly marked with Big Ears surveillance equipment, take their empty bellies home. It is just as Saori said. He furiously pulls out his phone.

"What's this rubbish all over the network? We've got Big Ears copters bombing the sleeper towns, for god's sake… What the hell is going on?"

"There's some kinda jam on the airwaves." His commander's voice is panicked. "We reckon it must be the new satellites. They're working on it, don't worry…" The phone crackles.

"So they've got through the fire walls."

"Indeed. There's a directive out for Safety Teams to close down public webscreens. Every bar, every shop window. By force if required. Are you onto that?"

"I will be. Number 31 has gone. I'm in her apartment." He is flicking through the channels. The screen shows a Safety Van ploughing into a mob of rescue workers. A Cool Sweat logo is shining from the doors.

"So is 33," his boss replies. "She reported recurring dreams to her mentor – does that mean anything?"

"What kind of dreams?"

"Er, kidnapped in the Patriotic War. Something about the er… I wrote it down… the year of man…Are you there? This year of man. I've heard that before. Remind me."

"It's a legend from a Northern cult," he replies, "rife in the eugenics factories. It refers to Madame X - remember her? – the missing committee member, who will return to finish the job in the final year of history, the Year of Man. It's, you know, an apocalypse myth."

"Right. What does it mean to us?"

"It means the abductees' depatterning might be breaking down."

"With all respect, officer, there are bigger problems tonight than a bunch of unravelling lab rats. We are going to have to blow the grid if this jamming doesn't stop."

Kovacs is not really listening because a new idea has dawned upon him. "Oh Lord… He says to himself.

"Kovacs?"

"Boss, This might be all connected."

"What?"

"31 and 33 might be sleepers…"

But the phone is dead. The connection has suddenly broken. He stares at it in surprise, and notices his Safety Team partner has been calling. He dials.

"Kovacs."

"What the fuck is going on?" The line is fading in and out.

"Have you found the old man?"

"Negative. There are new directives, you better get back…"

"I know. I want you to take them further. There may be enemy sleepers operating in the area. I want you to put everyone you see under house arrest. Get your helmets and tasers on and start closing down every webscreen in the neighbourhood. No questions – just enter every premises and pull the plug, and lock everyone in." He can hear a series of explosions from outside. "If anyone runs, shoot them." The line whistles. "What's happening now?"

"The microwaves towers are exploding…" He runs to the window. He sees sparks rising from distant buildings. He sees an airship, flaming to the ground. "Who is doing this? Who? Who?" Then he hears a woman's voice behind him. He spins around.

"In the centre of the town where my grandfather grew up…"

There is a cosmonaut on the screen, one blonde strand of hair waving around her head, reading about a clock tower. "I'll be there in a minute," he says into the now-dead phone. He sits down on the bed and looks at the screen, but doesn't get up.

*   *   *

I finally find a new belt – some boxing twine from a bin behind a supermarket. I tie it tight and clamber up a six metre high mound of turf, which is hemmed in between an apartment block and the supermarket. I crawl onto the top, push myself up, and look across the Imperial City. Warehouse walls are crossed by the blue-red flashes of emergency vehicles. Some distant towers are lit by flames. Sirens bleep everywhere. Blimps are adrift and streetlights flash emergency codes As I look at the night view, I increasingly feel I am in a kind of screen, a programme revealing some indigestible truth. Perhaps some new layer of the City's existence is being exposed. Seen from a star's perspective, or a satellite's, amongst the x-rays and circling years, these supermarkets and mansions are a mere blueprint. They rise and fall in an evolving pattern, much like the stars themselves. If this neighbourhood were vaporised tomorrow, or buried in a mound, a similar structure would soon arise, of the same materials, filled with people of roughly the same skills and appearances. Today's dead will be much like tomorrow's newborn, their hearts beating the same blood made of the same molecules by the same genes; the city's houses and factories would have the same functions. Is the world indeed a ghostly projection of some hidden program, a copy of something ancient, endlessly updated?

This mound I stand on is a case in point; it is the city's fate in miniature. It rarely receives a second glance from the shoppers and residents who shuffle past, assuming some dull municipal purpose to it - a sewage sump, a drainage reserve - yet it conceals an awful secret. Years ago I wrote an inscription for it that, for bureaucratic reasons, remains unread. Now is my chance: I stand up as straight as I can, take off my hat, and recite:

"In the twelfth year of his reign, The Emperor of Celestial Beauty began his mainland campaign to break the Siamese Dynasty's trading monopoly. To account for the heavy taxes imposed, he ordered his generals to count the number of slain enemy combatants. In order to achieve the task, the Generals ordered their troops to remove an ear from every Siamese soldier they killed. The troops set to work with gusto, and thousands of ears were soon shipped across the sea in barrels of vinegar, and brought to the feet of the Emperor.

"The Emperor gave the ears to his accountants, who then took them to the Shrines to be displayed to the citizens when they paid the required war tax of five copper coins. The coins were taken from the shrine collection boxes to the munitions factories where they were beaten into bullets and machines of war and shipped to the Siamese theatre, where the General's armies, now well-paid and well-supplied, worked frantically and without prejudice, lopping ears from women and children, old and young, farmers and shop-keepers, often not bothering to even kill the victim.

"So an economy of ears began. The shrines and munitions smelters reached full employment, the nation's coffers grew full, and the Siamese trading monopolies grew weaker and weaker. Yet, even as domestic markets boomed, the mood of the citizens changed. They began to shy away from the Shrines, so full were they of ears – and not just soldier's ears, and not just the ears of post officers and school children, but even the ears of pigs, which was a clear breach of the tax stipulations. On account of the expense and the spectacle, the smell of vinegar and rotting flesh, they demanded that the ears be buried, and that the buried ears be human ears only, preferably those of enemy combatants, or those that assist them.

"The Emperor hence employed a team of analysts to record the nature and proportion of each ear, and a team of legal experts to verify the origin of the same, and all the ears were tagged and buried in this mound as public verification. So the war continued in a more orderly and fiscally-responsible fashion, until the Siamese Empire was over-run, and their resources shared for the benefit of all."

I lift my top hat in salute. Ironically, the city around me now has ears in every window, ears in every bar, nook and cranny. The Big Ears logo is even stenciled on the wall of the supermarket next to me. There are layers of ears under every step, and Big Ears airships above, now falling, deaf. Standing upon the Mound of Ears, finally I understand my tiny role in the night's proceedings. The history of Imperial City in all its layers must be told, for if they can be exposed, the repeating illusion of history might stop.

I spin my cane and descend the Mound of Ears. Behind the supermarket is a dark canal. There is a ring-lock fence between me and it. I crawl between some rusty iron sheeting and climb down a service ladder. This canal once brought barges from the sea to the Emperor's Palace. Now it is a slime-infested ditch, overbuilt with apartment blocks and footbridges. It suits my purpose perfectly.

Shin-deep in oily brown muck, I wade downstream and freeze when a sound-truck crosses the bridge ahead. I scamper its dark tunnel, and listen to its tune tinkling across the neighbourhood, reminding us to go home, turn off the gas, pull the curtains tight. Perhaps it's Officer Kovacs looking for his girlfriend.

Somewhere nearby Saori is leaping between buildings, fearless and agile, scaling walls and ledges, threading a clandestine path above the city. Officer Kovacs is not entirely sure who she is anymore. Neither am I. Is she? Perhaps the cosmonaut's tale is true, and the children are climbing the rooves to herald the new sun.

The bridge I am sheltering under is built on old foundations. Below the graffiti-ed brick is a hand-hewn stone blocks engraved with faded characters. They are hard to read, unused for centuries, but inscribe the name of a goblin who once lived under this bridge: Kryraeth. It is, in a sense, one of the foundation stones of the City.

"Kryraeth the Goblin would not simply kill and devour passers-by," I recall, "but cruelly demand some terrible toll from them, such as the arm of their child, or the knees of their servant, which it would brutally extract and devour before them. Unable to defeat the demon, wayfarers into the City had to endure these atrocities in the only rational way: to bring them into the market. Orphans were sold to them as insurance against goblin attack. Should they be waylaid by Kryraeth, the child would be offered up, and as Kryraeth grew fatter, so did the City's orphan market. Brigands began to kidnap children from outlying villages to supply it; poverty fueled the market further as farmers and the urban poor sold extraneous issue for profit. Eventually the Emperor, in a rare moment of compassion, took pity on His citizens, and called upon a hero for assistance. The necromancer Lan Caihe flew from the mainland with his twelve enchanted swords and set to work. There was constant battle for a year. Kryraeth's curses twisted the swords into puzzling shapes; Lan Caihe reforged them with great fasts and mantras. Kryraeth fouled the air with toxic belches and farts that re-interned the spirits of the dead within the swords, so Lan Caihe was forced to call upon a magical ally, an immortal from the ancient days, whose mysterious sigils eventually bound the goblin's limbs, and innards. The necromancer then finished the job, grasping the eternal flame from a nearby temple and slowly burning the terrible monster alive. It is said Kryraeth's limbs boiled into liquid iron where they fell, and his blood turned the Grand Canal yellow for a decade."

I bow and clap again, and wade through the bridge's murky gloom. The Peach Boy jingle recedes, and I continue downstream. Next stop: the Silver Pavilion.

The canal soon passes a flight of stone steps leading out of the water to an old cracked gateway. The gate is sealed by two iron-plated oak doors lodged on copper hinges, and has a curved roof of cypress bark. The wood itself is dry and splintered, charred by successions of fires. I climb the steps and stand under it with water dripping from my tails, peering at butterflies and tigers, flowers and phoenixes decorating the panels with colour and gold. This is the neglected rear gate to the Silver Pavilion. Warming to my new role, I tell the story of how the great structure was built:

"Halfway through the One Hundred Years War, the Yellow Emperor returned from a period of fasting with an announcement that sent a sensation through the City: the Goddess of the Sun had ordered the construction of a giant brass bell which would redeem the sins of all citizens who helped build it. For full karmic effect, the bell should be housed in a pavilion of pure silver, and it must be the largest bell in the world, uniting the realms of heaven and earth with its pure and harmonious tones. This offer was too good to refuse, and every neighbourhood militia ceased fire and began to melt down all their pikes and guns, their bronze armour and cannons, their daggers and shields and donate the metal to the smelters. The destructive war ceased overnight; the rich melted down their candlesticks and spoons; the poor their belt buckles and buttons and while the populace laboured, the City remained peaceful.

"The Emperor rejoiced – his ruse had worked! Yet there was a problem: an actress famous for her beauty, called Oe, regretted donating her precious bronze mirror to the smelter. This treasure had been handed down through generations of her family, and as soon as she had given it to the Emperor's metal collectors, she longed and pined to look again into its priceless face, which reflected not just her, but all the roles she played, and all the roles played by all the players in her ancestry. Her deep attachment to the mirror stayed fixed within the metal that was mixed into the huge bell, and weakened it.

"After two years the bell was hung in its beautiful pavilion. The stupendous monument shone like a star for miles around, attracting worshippers and admirers from all over the nation. Every morning and evening the Emperor came out of his palace and struck the bell himself, and peace reigned as its beautiful tone echoed across the fields, now re-sprouting with crops and buildings, trade and children. No-one heard the slight impurity in the bell's pitch, the subtle almost imperceptibly off tone – no-one except Oe. Every time she heard the bell struck, she didn't rejoice with the other citizens, or think of her coming eternity in heaven, but felt bitterly the loss of her dearest possession. She could not forget the image of herself in the mirror's depths, or the respect she had for her family tradition, while on stage she lost the confidence and charm the mirror had given her, and hence her livelihood. Her loss and regret grew heavier and heavier and eventually, with each sounding of the bell, the metal weakened from the points her pining reached, until one morning the giant bell split in two and crashed from its ropes onto the floor of the pavilion and broke into a thousand pieces.

"The citizens rushed to witness the terrible event. As they were already ensured of an eternity free of sin, they also rushed to reclaim the metals it scattered, and – with no need to repair the bell – they sold them back to the warlords, who forged them back into cannons and axes and pistols. The city was once again re-armed and divided, and the militias – now convinced of their moral purity and eternal seat in heaven – recommenced the vicious war which continued for several decades."

I clap my hands and bow, then peer through the gate at the ancient pavilion. It is a majestic sight, a giant lozenge of silver magnifying the starlight from above, its horned rooves rising in a milky glow. The Tanabata stars are now moving into the western sky, slowly fizzing into the roof's peak, melting and dripping down its silver tiles, but its proportions reflect a more invisible light – that of the numbers of life. The building is a vestige of a time when religion, mathematics and architecture were the same. The priests who designed it encoded primal fractions into its frame: the equations of growth and decay to which all life conforms. It stands in the city yet seems to float above it; a broken symmetry connecting earth to sky, matter to mind, animal to cosmos, and for a second I feel I have left the city and am approaching a place where all things are briefly in step.

I watch a monk walking quickly along a wooden balcony. His steps create a rhythmic squeaking, from deliberately loose nails, so that people can monitor movement throughout the complex. His face is glowing, not with divinity but from his mobile phone. Is he watching the cosmonaut's tale? He climbs down some steps, slips on a pair of straw sandals and crosses the garden, face still glued to the screen. When he gets to a small teahouse he snaps closed his phone, bends down and pulls two blue plastic containers from under the balcony. He walks back along the stone pathway, taking tight steps in his robes and sandals, and climbs up to the alcove of the main pavilion. There he unscrews one container and begins to empty the liquid inside onto the ancient floorboards. He sets off around the wooden balcony and in five minutes has circled the entire pavilion. The boards are now silent, soaked in kerosene.

At the base of the steps, a blue cloud of musky incense smoke gushes permanently from the mouth of a large dragon. The monk descends to this urn, takes a burning stick and, after a brief but reverent bow, tosses it up to the balcony.

The effect is dramatic. Two balls of blue fire run in both directions around the Pavilion, lighting up the paper doors and racing up the wooden pillars. Within seconds the bell chamber is encased in a wall of orange flame, and chains of black smoke billow outwards. The monk backs away into the garden, transfixed by his handiwork. The inferno roars, draws air, pops rivets as silver plate gives way to the timber structure within. Sparks and charred fragments blow out. I can feel the heat on my face even through the gap in the gate. Shouts ring out. Lights flicker on in other buildings. The arsonist has withdrawn to the shadows at the back of the garden and is standing only metres in front of me.

"Excuse me," I call to him and he turns to investigate my cries. "You can hide up in the gate! There are secret platforms where soldiers used to hide, to ambush unexpected visitors." He walks right up to me. He looks calm, not frightened.

"I don't want to escape or hide," he replies. "I want to celebrate. I want everyone to know the great deed I have done."

I laugh. "Celebrate? What kind of monk destroys the City's most glorious attraction?"

"I'm not destroying it." he shakes his head with a thin smile. "I am demonstrating its eternity."

I squint at him through the gate.

"The structure will be remade," he explains, "from the template conceived by the Sun Goddess hundreds of years ago. Its perfect form will be renewed. Its current form is in decay, transient and departing, as you can see. Its eternal form is a structure of unchanged information, locked in the Imperial palace. A new copy will emerge as the old one collapses. Same form, different substance. As my lessons have taught me: how else can the universe remain eternal, without renewing itself every moment?"

Alarm bells start to sound from within the compound. More robed figures appear.

"You'll be arrested for certain. They'll think you are a Northern agent, a sleepwalker."

He nods enthusiastically. "So it should be. On this plane of fear and attachment, it would be a fitting response to a person who does this. There's nothing that can change that."

Three senior monks run up behind him, shouting in panic and anger. "You'll be pilloried," I say, " thrown in the flames." Crashing and splintering sounds come from the hall.

"I hope so." The three monks grab him by the arms and begin dragging him back toward the buildings. He gives little resistance. The first fire officers sprint through the front entrance, dragging hoses from the street. I don't want to see his fate, nor risk mine, so turn away. Was he watching the cosmonaut's tale before he committed his crime? Is he acting under the coded command of satellites orbiting above?

Across the city half a dozen steeples of smoke are rising – more buildings on fire. Are there others like him, torching the monuments of Imperial City? As I said before, this is one city buried under another, and now under the spell of the Tanabata tale, or the sweep of a satellite's orbit, the current facsimile is collapsing.

Safety Teams, with riot shields and tasers, are now running into the Pavilion grounds. Gone are their happy melodies – they start kicking in doors, raiding dormitories, sectioning off buildings. I can hear them dragging away several monks, who are shouting their horror and surprise. I stay dead still, feeling an itching around my heart, listening to jets roar in the distance, while webscreens are smashed, people beaten, furniture overturned.

Such scenes, as the monk hinted, have been an historical constant. I remember what Marco Polo said: *"Hitmen is a better word."* Knights of this or that Order. Special Forces. Protectors of the rich. They always wear sigil crests of geometric patterns, are always guarding the temples, high streets and banks –wherever the money is. They always cloak themselves behind the morals of political freedom or religion - they often quote such authorities - but are essentially the arms of criminal organisations incorporated as states. The ones I saw burning the Saint and her followers created, in the fifteenth century, the world's first fully-functioning police state, and for centuries my nation has lived under some form of martial law. Every neighbourhood and workplace is under the surveillance of a network of gatekeepers: highly educated men, of stature, letters and breeding, professions loyal to landowners and businessmen. They draw curtains around the public lives of citizens, who withdraw to personal pursuits and ambitions. So great entertainments drive the economy. We are drawn to pleasure quarters that thrive on fads and hedonism. Web are entertained by goals and spectacles which screen us from the divided state of our souls. Our society has become exiled from reality; a fantasy world where desires are manufactured and satisfied in a constant stream of programmes and images. We are consumer-peasants in a corporate state, and strange beliefs spread: we are a free society; everyone is equal; other nations hate us because we are good. Our government has an historical, possibly divine purpose. After hundreds of years of this kind of exile, the citizens of Imperial City literally live within a fiction, a manufactured reality.

It is time to sneak away from the Silver Pavilion. It's crawling with police, and getting dangerously late – I must meet the Emperor at dawn. I spin my cane and scamper down the steps, through the shadows to the canal. From here it is lined with

flagpoles down to the Imperial Palace: the Royal
Mile.

Imperial flags, prefectural flags, school flags, flags
with sun rays and moon crescents, mascot flags and
corporate flags, Peach Boy flags and Big Ears flags,
American flags and European flags, flags with
flowers and famous faces and fast food, pub flags
and car flags, flags of the corporate brotherhoods –
Saturn's rings, goat's horns, owl's masks; flags with
mathematical and alchemical symbols - all flying in
the night sky. I pause in surprise - flying amongst
them, amazingly, unmistakably - is the flag of the
North. The unclosed black circle, the brutal mark of
slavery is flying up there amongst all the global
symbols of freedom and prosperity. There are quite a
few of them scattered amongst the display, like
rotten apples in a tree. This is a first. The Northern
flag hasn't been seen in the South for a generation.
Is there some kind of diplomatic visit in the middle
of the launch crisis? A sudden breakthrough in
détente? Or is it some further infection from the
network, one layer reflecting another? I keep wading
through the murky canal. I must get to the Palace as
fast as I can. I continue my tale to stay alert:

"Heartbroken at the resumption of the Hundred
Years War, the Yellow Emperor returned to his
fasting, and the now silent pavilion became a
playpen for the political elite. While the city outside
tore itself to shreds, they held garden parties and tea
ceremonies. They built lavish villas in its grounds
and staffed them with their mistresses and spies.
Under the peach blossoms, warlords curried

influence with scholars, and scholars with priests, and priests with bureaucrats, so the warlords donned the cloak of moral intelligence, and the priests supplied funds to the rulers, and the elite had an army to defend their business interests. The pavilion became a training facility for public service, and military control developed under the cloak of religious faith.

"One of the acolytes of the Pavilion was Charlemagus, a religious general who united the east and west of the city and ended the Hundred Year War. He brokered a power-sharing deal between the warlords and the nobles, and by the time they had finished, the streets of the Imperial City were littered with corpses. The Imperial seat was a smoking ruin. The throne itself was a perch for monkeys and birds; the family members were reduced to beggars who thrust their arms through the palace walls, soliciting soldiers who passed by. Charlemagus lined the highway from the Port to the City with the heads of sectarian soldiers as a warning to those who would divide the hearts and minds of the citizens again.

"He then threw the borders of the nation open to the world. The myopic age of the Emperors was over. Decadence and class exploitation would give way to reason and industry. The world's emissaries arrived to marvel at the brand new nation. The new President was heralded as a great peacemaker, a modernizer, a revolutionary, He ushered in a period of cultural flowering and economic growth which culminated in the invasion of the mainland, and the division of the homeland."

Logos of food brands and baseball teams, motor cars and perfumes, fantasies and superstars, glitter and distraction: there are no heads lining the Royal Mile tonight: instead they display the symbols of our occupation, how our minds and lives have been occupied, not just by revolution but by profit and commodity, sensation and privilege, all the things that have divided us from each other. Up there tonight flies the dreaded Northern flag. Will the divided states combine? Will the black circle of history be drawn? Is this how the Year of Man will dawn?

If the long dreamed-of unification of my country ever happens, it will not be some wonderful civic or psychological state, because the basis of our separation is fear, fear of giving up what we know. In a world where every individual is divided from the other, unification will be a bitter and painful trial of giving up everything we have to embrace the wrong, the opposite, and the hated.

The roof of the Silver Pavilion behind me falls in. I feel the sound first then the shockwave. The bridges shake. Burning cinders blow all around, hissing in the water. Sirens start to wail and the sound of boots running across the bridge: soldiers now, not just Safety Officers. Armoured personnel carriers are rolling down the streets and tracers are zipping from the rooves, from snipers taking up positions in nearby buildings. It would seem the curfew has morphed into martial law.

I can only pray my black tails and hat provide some camouflage as I walk these last few hundred metres through the murky canal, and it helps that the water itself black, as the sewage pipes have burst. Lumps of shit and streaks of brown tissue are swirling around my legs. Plastic bags and cans, clumps of food and hair, even more pollution seems to be joining the flow: sections of appliances, leaking toxins, years of stuck garbage is bubbling up from decaying pipes. Fuller and fuller the waters become: all that once filled the screens and airwaves, the shop windows and magazines, all the attractive products in their perfect packages are now bubbling up as a digested mess, mixed up and heading for oblivion.

If I were an Emperor, or a monk, I might try to wipe this river clean, return everything to its original pure state, but I wade with it, a part of it, the dirt of the smokestacks and houses, a decrepit old man, my tails ruined, my body being expelled from the city along with all its other toxins. This Tanabata night is ending in a giant purge.

Finally I see the walls of the Imperial palace looming above the other buildings. The blank walls are a masterpiece of design: a quiet face concealing a hidden and private world. As such, it reflects the national personality, alluring yet hiding more than it reveals. What is behind the wall? No-one really knows. The Emperor and his family only ever appear outside their gardens dressed in tails and gowns at official functions, surrounded by bouquets of flowers. Their real lives are closed off to public scrutiny.

I climb out of the canal, sodden and stinking, and stare at the edifice above me. It also reflects the social system that surrounds it – the ugly facts of self or nation, the truth and the secrets within, are screened away like contraband.

I've known it from the first word of tonight's tale - soon I am going to meet the Emperor, and find out what he really is. Tonight Imperial City's long upheld appearances are failing, and the world behind the imposing facade of the Palace walls will be revealed.

I can see the red glow of fires. Satellites are broadcasting dissonant data. Airships and choppers flash lights and slogans through the pre-dawn sky:

Listen to the Children
Running Through the Night

I can hear a hubbub of yells like a distant waterfall. People must be waking up in fright and confusion, and gathering on the streets. I stop in front of the Eastern gate – not an iron-studded barrier but a modern steel façade, polished and seamless. I expect a sound truck to turn one of the distant corners soon, and motor my way, bristling with armed guards. I bow and clap my hands and tell the night's final story:

"When Charlemagus triumphed as the last remaining warlord, he knew the ancient days were over. He could now usher in his long-planned reforms. After opening the borders and saving the nation from its corrupt traditions, he gathered the royal bloodlines together and built for them a great new palace in the centre of the city, and surrounded it with wide gardens. He built it with fountains of milk and wine and floors of gold; he installed windows of crystal and doors studded with gems; he ordered wagons loaded with the finest products of the land – cheeses and chocolates, silks and cloths, liqueurs and fruits, courtesans and scholars – through its gates every day. Exiled from rule and realm, the Imperial Dynasty passed its time in the pursuit of pleasure – poetry and music, boating and games, debates with philosophers, masquerades and balls in the moonlit glades or picnics beside the carp-stocked lakes, fireworks and jugglers and orgiastic parties attended by the most beautiful men and women in the country. The royal family lived inside a sealed and seamless pleasure dome, and for centuries no-one heard of or saw these ancient kings and queens, for no-one who entered this Palace could ever leave. There were merely rumours of the sunny world within its towers and walls, and brief glimpses of its hypnotic splendours.

"Charlemagus' ruse was even cleverer than his predecessors': he simultaneously restored the majesty and status of the royal line, yet stripped them of all power and importance. His true political genius, however, was how he then applied it to his subjects outside the Palace walls. His newly-liberated nation became a secular, global garden for its citizens. Their pleasures and freedoms were exalted, and the glory of their humanity was turned in on itself with a lurid, self-satisfying gaze.

"Charlemagnus created ministers to enact his visions, parliaments to manage the acts; industries to enrich the people, and armies to protect the profits. His elected ministers became demagogues, and his institutions became egalitarian walls, screening away the warlords' power from scrutiny. Inside the City there was total freedom and satisfaction; its people believed they governed themselves and the world around them, and nature itself was yoked to provide an endless stream of luxuries and products. But they were in fact still prisoners who could not leave. They had become just like the venerated emperors and empresses of old, who were ostracized and stripped of power and influence inside their crystal pleasure dome."

There is no more time. I lift up my walking cane, and bang its tiger's head grip firmly in the centre of the giant steel door. Three metallic retorts ring out, and out of the corners of my eyes I see movement at the ends of the walls. In the north a cloud of dust is swirling; from the south comes the roar of engines. I turn to see a fleet of personnel carriers rounding the corner, bristling with the barrels of weapons and the domes of helmets. But there is a another sound – a kind of thunder, like a stampeding herd of beasts.

All that has been put in train tonight is reaching a culmination. Is the Emperor in his Palace or is it just an empty shell? I lift up my cane and bang again on the door: "Open!" I demand. "Open up! The city is awake!"

There's a deafening roar and huge lights streak just metres over the top of the wall. I slip to my knees in the grey gravel as jet afterburners streak away to the north. There are other jets buzzing over the city, glinting brightly in the sunlight. The sun hasn't yet reached our patch of earth, but it won't be long. Below the dawn-lit clouds blimps are displaying absurd warnings:

Step into the new and we will
fill the gap in your heart.

Amongst all the sirens and jets I can hear the source of the hubbub that is streaming around the northern walls - and it is not human. It is a cacophony of grunts, barks and squeals. Horns and snouts are approaching, hooves and trotters are raising dust, manes and stripes are colouring the gloom. All the creatures under the sun are arriving at the Palace door, and it looks like I have been the first.

The military trucks brake to a dusty stop and soldiers fan out in an organised drill across the gravel. Immediately the formation starts to falter as the beasts swarm across the square: cats, rodents and fowl, meercats and wolverines are getting under the soldiers' feet. A tiger lopes singularly, a troop of monkeys start to climb the wall. The soldiers aren't sure what to do. Some aim in confusion at the horses, the tapirs; some more disciplined units drop to their knees and train their weapons on me.

I lift my hands up in submission, still on my knees, and look at the even larger crowd of citizens stretching behind the animals. Their flags are white and empty, and the their presence is simply the amplified murmur of breath, the quiet awareness of a million people released from a spell.

"Freeze!" The army commander's voice is pumped through a megaphone. Ammunition rounds are clicked home. Cats and rats run everywhere. Spotlights flash from the back of the jeeps, lighting up faces with halogen rays in the pre-dawn gloom.

The elephant trumpets. The cow moos. The people keep marching. There is a woman leading the crowd, and she's holding what appears to be a wand, or a bit of electronic equipment: Saori's makeshift transmitter. The woman's face is face beautiful, symmetric, but it is not Saori's face: it is marred with bruises, or a birthmark - fatal flaws to a near-perfect beauty.

"Stop your approach!"

She begins to drag her feet, perhaps to baffle the commanders. Her hand curls, stiffens, and I really do freeze as I realise I have seen this trick before: sixty years ago, as a soldier kneeling on the floor of my commandant's quarters, as my first lover stole from me with his sword. Rebel, fake, revolutionary hero – the woman leading the crowd onwards is Mei Li, here again, alive.

"Stop Your Advance!"

The soldiers' elbows are shaking as they train their weapons on her but she does not stop on the commander's order – she stops before me. The huge crowd stops too, and a sudden silence falls. I am kneeling with my hands upraised, Mei Lee looking intently into my eyes with a hint of recognition. I know exactly who you are, she seems to say.

Black columns rise into the sky. Flying blades chop through them. I sense a slight shudder underfoot, like heavy machinery passing on a highway. Then silence returns - the sound of a million people waiting. Mei Li turns to face the guards. Behind their armoured suits and perspex shields, I can sense enormous uncertainty about what to do next.

"I order you to disperse!" The commander shouts. "Go back to your homes."

Saori raises her fist silently into the air. The row of flags lining the canal are now lit orange by the rising sun. The lion roars. Another shudder rattles the steel gate behind me.

"Drop your fist!"

The monkeys chatter. The tiger leaps into a tree. There is a muffled explosion, and the door shakes again. It seems to have come from inside the palace. Is this the answer to my knock? The tops of the pines lining the square are now lit orange. The animals are calling furtively – mice are climbing the soldiers' bodies, spiders are swarming across the stones.

Then it's as if a mountain falls over. An almighty jolt tilts the earth from side to side. People stumble and fall, I look behind me: a crack of light has appeared in the centre of the palace door. Saori is standing firm, fist raised in salute.

"Behold! The Emperor approaches!" She declares. "Look who has won the race to his door," her other hand is stretching back to point at me. "A man! Man is time's champion!"

Something heavy breaks away from the door. The paving cracks. Light floods from within the Palace and casts my shadow, like an ape's, across the gravel up to the feet of the first row of troops. I see some of them backing away. Their commander bellows: "Stand your ground!"

There is another huge rumble, and the ground tilts terrifyingly again, sending people and animals reeling. The mice swarm up the tree trunks. A crack forms in the Palace walls. Streams of orders issue from radios in the trucks. Saori stands firm:

"Bow down before the Emperor!" She demands.

I can feel extreme heat on my back and the soles of my feet. An intense light is streaming from the door, washing out the army spotlights. I am crawling away from the source, scrabbling for handholds; the world lifts vertiginously; and the circular scar around my heart burns.

The commanding officer yells something more but no-one is listening. All are looking behind me at the door. There are gasps and howls and squeals of amazement.

"Behold!" Saori demands. "Hold your fire and behold the Year of Man!"

I look up at her, and her face has changed for the last time. The dark birthmarks on her face have broken and separated and are becoming scales. The kimono I bought her has grown a surface of feathers, and her crooked limbs have bent into claws and wings. Then I notice what I should have noticed before - the crowd of people around her is not from the City at all. They are not disenchanted citizens standing up to the state, nor an insurgent mob under the sway of a cult leader. They are wearing the costumes of the ages – skins and kaftans, silk gowns and waistcoats, top hats and ponchos, and they are not just linking hands and arms, but are joined from limb to limb, connected by flesh, melded together into one great single body. As I look further into this crowd, this continuous body doesn't stop with the people, but includes the animals too. The human faces stretch into snouts and whiskers, their bodies into talons and tails – there is no creature that is separate here, all that has ever been born and died are emerging and held inside one another in a chain of being, a dividing cell that grows out of itself. And this crowd screams in one voice, a grand electric chorus of a many octaves: "It is the Year of Man! The Year of Man!"

And I bow. I bow down deeply before my maker, frail and weak, prostrate and submitted, a part of its body, attached to it by these nails of flesh, about to be consumed by its light, as the commander brings his arms defiantly down.

*   *   *

It was then, as the bullets left the soldiers' guns, that I remembered what happened under the Marco Polo Bridge years ago. The memory flooded back into my mind like a light-beam, filling the dark hole that had been there for sixty years, and re-connecting me with my life. I was back under the Marco Polo bridge, when I had left my company and fallen down to awake into a dream that I have been having ever since.

I walked across the rocks towards the mysterious voice singing under the bridge. Fireworks were exploding all around. The long stone curve of the bridge divided the starry sky above, where Vega and Altair approached each other, two points in the summer triangle. Fireflies looped and circled in the humid air like tiny green lamps. I could hear the voices of my commanding officer as he shouted orders to my comrades behind me. I followed the spritely voice, modulating three tones above the roar of the river, weaving notes between the retorts of the shells.

Under the bridge, amongst the rocks, was the faint glow of a fire. A figure with black hair was seated there. My heart leapt – it was Mei Lee! I was still steeped in the warm glow of our sexual union. I felt in my pocket for the turtle-shell comb she had left – I wanted to see her slide it into her hair again. I wanted to see her whole and real, not the crippled persona, cross-eyed and false. I forgot her fateful warnings. I walked towards her, entranced, my feet crunchy on the river stones. The voice was silky and pure, like running water.

Of course it was a trap. As I passed a small boulder two men leapt out. I struggled and shouted, in full view of the bridge above, but the fireworks were exploding, camouflaging their ambush. I was punched, muffled, and dragged toward the fire where Mei Li had stopped singing and was waiting for me. She was grinning in a menacing way.

"My little servant, my faithful one," she said sympathetically. "I told you not to follow me." They bound me with thick wet rope. I knew her words were an elegy. Mei Li walked up to the fire and lifted Yamamoto's sword - its blade was white hot. She held it aloft – it illuminated her glittering gaze, which refocused from the sword to my eyes. We studied each other's features, faces almost touching. I found the blue congenital bruises under her skin more attractive than the flawless complexion I had imagined.

"Stupid boy," she said and ran her fingers around my cheekbones, "out of control of his fate." There was nothing left in the world but the fireworks in her eyes, the complex beauty of multi-hued skin. Red blue green shadows rippled up and down her long hair. She slid her fingers between the buttons of my khaki shirt and wrenched them away.

"Stupid boy," she repeated, "now fate has chosen you." With the swift determination of a practiced surgeon, she wielded the sword and cut a circle around my heart. The blood sprayed and my spine arched. The flesh fell back. She bent down and peered inside my chest as if it were an interesting compartment she had found. I stopped breathing and my body started to empty.

Then two things happened. First, Hei Jin stepped from behind a rock, brandishing a rifle. He looked terrified, and gestured wildly at me. I couldn't hear any words coming from his lips, but he seemed to want to help me. Secondly, Mei Li, with eyes shining like lamps, dropped the sword. Weakened by fire, it broke in half with a clatter.

Great jets were pumping out of me. I was bleeding fatally. Mei Li put her fingers inside the hole in my chest, then her hands, and Hei Jin began shooting. Bullets sheared off the rocks. Ricochets and retorts blended with the bursts of fireworks.

Now the borders between these two moments in history have become blurred. The layers of time are shifting, re-aligning, blending. I am simultaneously kneeling in the blaze of the Emperor, facing the bullets of the Southern army, while kneeling under the Marco Polo bridge, facing the rifle of Hei Jin. Mei Li stood before me then, and stands inexplicably before me again. History is repeating, but not exactly in the same way. I realise there has never really been any escape from this moment – I have always been in it. It always exists.

I have lost possession of my body, which is in an apposite state of panic – involuntary spasms rise up through me as Mei Li reaches further inside my chest with her arms, soaking in my blood. Then she puts her head in. The feeling is not pain but exquisite pleasure.

Hei Jin is a toy soldier, tiny and distant, frozen in position, just like the army troops, spraying bullets which bounce of the rocks and palace walls as harmlessly as water drops. Mei Lee works her way into my body; first her shoulders, then her back, then her hips, lubricated by blood, then her feet lift as she slides down seemingly from the stars, through the sword-carved hole, into my body.

Silence.

The firing has stopped. Hei Jin and Mei Li have disappeared. The troops and animals have gone. The crowd of people is absent. There is just the Emperor left, and the only movement is the river, eternal and pure, flowing out of him and into the City, under the bridges, past the shrines and factories, through the fields and over the plain, bringing the world alive, a river of consciousness with one heart, one source, one singular being high above all, embracing.

The End

Acknowledgments

The author thanks the following people for their
invaluable help and support in finishing this novel:
Burke Bridgman, Alex Trouchet, Robin Trouchet,
Mariko Dammacco, Chris Irwin, Brooke Suzuki,
Griselda Hitchcock, Ikuko Nakaji,
Noah Nakaji-Hitchcock.

If you would like to discuss this work
with the author, please check for the title
and author on social networking sites.